Have you heard the gossip about Pierre's other books?

Maple Springs

"*Maple Springs* is a really fun read. The pacing is just right, the characters are interesting and unique, and a few unexpected twists kept me turning the pages. A well done horror-thriller that is light on the gore, heavy on surprises. Awesome!" – Author Rebecca MacFarlane

"I really enjoyed this story. A bit spooky and lots of suspense. Arseneault is a fine storyteller." – Author Allan Hudson

Dark Tales for Dark Nights

"A great collection of horror shorts by two talented authors. As a horror fan, I highly recommend it!" – Author Cassandra L. Thompson

Poplar Falls: The Death of Charlie Baker

"Arseneault is a clever storyteller who fills his tale with subplots that diverge and frequently intersect as his narrative unwinds." – Joe Kilgore – The US Review of Books

"An entertaining whodunit that takes readers on a sometimes graphic, often naughty adventure featuring a wide cast of colourful characters. Full of surprises, this is a lighthearted story, well told!" – Eden Monroe, author of *Dare To Inherit* and *Gold Digger Among Us*.

"A highly entertaining story. Charlie Baker is a unique character, his untimely death and the shenanigans in *Poplar Falls* will keep you intrigued to the very end. There are some laugh-out-loud moments making the story even more enjoyable." – Author Allan Hudson

"Pierre will definitely keep you guessing until the very

end. If you're looking for something fresh, with a hint of naughty, this is the book for you." – Author Lina Gardiner

Oakwood Island
"If you're a fan of good old-fashioned death, blood and gore, like Stephen King books and mystery - this is a must read!" – Author Sarah Butland

Oakwood Island: The Awakening
"This is a horror/thriller that I would gladly recommend." – Author Yves Robichaud

Other Books by Pierre C. Arseneault
Sleepless Nights
Poplar Falls: The Death of Charlie Baker
Maple Springs

Other Books by Angella Cormier and Pierre C. Arseneault
Dark Tales for Dark Nights
Oakwood Island
Oakwood Island: The Awakening

As Part of Anthologies
Autumn Paths
Winter Paths
Spring Paths
Summer Paths

SOMETHING HAPPENED IN CARLTON

By
Pierre C Arseneault

Artemesia
Publishing

ISBN: 978-1-963832-10-5 (paperback)
ISBN: 978-1-963832-25-9 (ebook)
LCCN: 2024951569
Copyright © 2025 by Pierre C. Arseneault
Cover Illustration and Design © 2025 Ian Bristow

Printed in the United States

Names, characters, and incidents depicted in this book are products of the author's imagination or are used fictitiously. Any resemblance to actual events, locales, organizations, or persons, living or dead, is entirely coincidental and beyond the intent of the author or the publisher.

All rights reserved. No part of this book may be reproduced or transmitted in any form or by any means, electronic or mechanical, including photocopying, recording, or by any information storage or retrieval system without written permission of the publisher, except for the inclusion of brief quotations in a review.

NO AI TRAINING: Without in any way limiting the author's [and publisher's] exclusive rights under copyright, any use of this publication to "train" generative artificial intelligence (AI) technologies to generate text is expressly prohibited. The author reserves all rights to license uses of this work for generative AI training and development of machine learning language models.

Artemesia Publishing
9 Mockingbird Hill Rd
Tijeras, New Mexico 87059
www.apbooks.net
info@artemesiapublishing.com

For Diane Comeau.
Thinking of you.

Introduction

IN THE BEGINNING, THE WORKING title for this book was simply Carlton. About a third of the way into writing this book, the actual title came to me. I knew I had to change the title to *Something Happened in Carlton*. Now with that said, I feel I need to explain the title of this book, in case your memory is fuzzy or perhaps you've never read my earlier short story collection, *Sleepless Nights*. Said collection had the first stories set in the small town of Carlton. Even if not yet in Carlton, you meet one of its residents briefly in the very first story called 'Subliminal'. In the third story, I bring you to Carlton for the very first time. A story called 'Sleepy Meadows'. Here you met more of the townsfolk. Later in that book, I bring you back there in a story called 'Speechless'. Then for the last story in the book, I introduced to you much of the cast in this book. That story bears the title, 'Nothing Ever Happens in Carlton'. This is how many of the residents of the quiet little town felt as life was generally uneventful and peaceful in the beloved yet boring little community. At least that was how they felt back then.

With that said, the reason I began writing this book to begin with were feelings of nostalgia and a longing to return to a beloved place that was very special to me. There are places we cherish, these feelings growing stronger with the passage of time. Those unique special places somehow worm their ways into our hearts and minds. Perhaps it's the time spent there, or the emotions said place brings out in us as we reminisce about what this place meant to us when last we visited. I've also wondered if it isn't the people and not only the place that makes us feel that way. The bonds made and moments shared. But often we can't deny the strong emotions and sentimental memories increasing our desires to return to said place and create new memories.

Quite often, as readers we find ourselves feeling this way about fictional places even more so than real places. And the same can be said for authors as well. We often long to return to places we've created and spend more time with the people we put there.

So now here we are again, about to enter the town limits of a little place called Carlton. Population 1236, if you don't include the outskirts of town in that total, that is. A place I've been longing to return to for a while. And if this is your first time in the small, charming fictional town of Carlton, then I hope your heart grows as fond of the place as mine has. Unless you've read *Sleepless Nights*, then you've already been to Carlton and were already introduced to many of its residents. Either way, I want to welcome you, whether it's your first time or a return trip, to spend time with both old and new friends alike. So, join me as we wander through Carlton and spend time with its residents.

Prologue

"*It's been a while since* you've been in to see me," Doctor Evee Melanson said to Libby who sat on the couch across from the doctor's chair.

Officer Libby Terwilliger picked a few black cat hairs off her jeans which she wore with a plain white shirt that while feminine, gave her an all-business appearance. The stray cat had rubbed up against her as she left for her appointment.

A feeling of guilt made Libby tuck the cat hairs into a pants pocket while marveling at how Doctor Melanson kept her office neat. She kept the room where she met patients even neater. They had discussed this on Libby's first visit, years ago. How Doctor Melanson liked to control the environment which helped keep her patients from getting distracted during sessions.

Specializing in trauma, Doctor Melanson was referred patients from all types of fields, including law enforcement.

"How have you been?" Doctor Melanson inquired.

"Good," Libby replied.

"Still squeamish?"

Libby made a seesawing gesture with her hand, miming her answer.

"What does that mean?" Doctor Melanson pried.

"I don't do well with the sight of blood. Not that I did all that well before, but now it's much worse."

"Worse how?"

Libby stiffened as she spoke. "If I see anything more than a papercut, I get woozy."

Doctor Melanson wrote as Libby continued.

"I feel like I'm going to pass out."

"Do you? Pass out?"

"Sometimes," Libby replied while looking down at the coffee table before her.

"It's nothing to be ashamed of," Doctor Melanson stated. "Do you feel it affects your job in law enforcement?"

"Not really," Libby replied making eye contact. "It's not like I'm a paramedic or something."

Doctor Melanson took notes.

"Not that I could have ever been one in the first place. I've always been uncomfortable with blood, unless it's my own. But since the…the…incident…" Libby said, trailing off.

"The incident at Burnett's Place?" Doctor Melanson asked.

Libby nodded, "But that's not why I wanted to come here. Not this time."

"So, tell me why you wanted to see me again?" Doctor Melanson asked as she turned to a fresh page in her notebook.

"Where do I start?" Libby muttered. She tucked her hands under her thighs and cast her gaze down as if deep in thought. "We hired someone since we last spoke. Officer Keirstead. He's a big boy. Almost doesn't fit in the cruiser."

"And how do you feel about that?" Doctor Melanson asked.

Libby blushed as she spoke. "About him being a big guy?"

"I don't know, you tell me," Doctor Melanson replied.

"Or do you mean about hiring him in the first place? I mean I like him. I'm glad we hired him. He's a good cop. But it's the why we hired him that bothers me the most."

"Tell me about that," Doctor Melanson pushed. "Tell me about what's bothering you."

"You heard, right?" Libby asked.

"Heard?"

"About the Chief?"

"Let's assume not," Doctor Melanson stated.

"It must be weird for you," Libby said. "Talking to someone about their trauma before it even happens."

"I suppose it is," Doctor Melanson replied. "Tell me how all of this makes you feel."

Part 1

Trash Talk

1

UNDER A CLEAR BLUE SKY, with a blend of coniferous and deciduous trees at his back, his police cruiser parked in a long dirt driveway off Short Fir Road, Police Chief Clovis McPhee stood in the crook of the open door of the cruiser. His arms rested on the roof and open door as he waited for a response on the police radio. After a moment of only static, he radioed again.

"Libby? Reggie? You over at Eli Woodman's place yet? Over."

After another moment's wait, the radio crackled to life as Officer Terwilliger responded.

"We're at the Woodman residence now. Over."

"Everything good over there? Over."

"His truck's in the driveway and Eli's in his house," Libby radioed. "We can see him watching us from the living room window. Otherwise, all seems quiet here. Over."

Chief Clovis shifted his stance and stifled a smile as he replied. Poetic justice often had that effect on him, but he struggled not to show it. Chances where good Garth Blackett was watching him from inside his home as well.

"I'm gonna go chat with Garth now. Over."

"Okay," Libby replied. "Reggie and I are going to go talk to Mr. Woodman. Over and out."

"Copy that. Over and out."

Clovis racked the radio mike, scooped up his police-issue baseball cap, and put it on over his predominantly graying hair. He shut the cruiser door and limped up to Blackett's crew cab truck, pausing to assess the situation. The reason Garth called in the first place.

The doors to Garth's truck had been opened wide and strewn inside the cab as well as the truck bed, overflowing to the gravel driveway around the vehicle, was garbage. Most were black plastic trash bags with some blue and clear ones in the mix. Many had been torn open to spew their contents. Clovis could see flies buzzing around Skipper Jack's Pizza boxes, cardboard coffee cups from the local Santorene coffee shop, empty silver beer cans, plastic wrappers and bags, empty food cans and various other trash. Sticking out of the pile on the driver's side, was a handful of discarded papers including enough junk mail to give a mail carrier a hernia. From it, Clovis plucked out one of the clear windowed envelopes and examined it. He tucked it into his back pocket, adjusted his gun belt and limped towards the modest Blackett home as the front door opened. Clovis casually unsnapped his Taser holster but left the weapon where it was, at the ready. Garth had a temper and Clovis didn't feel up to hand-to-hand combat, if that's what it came down to.

"Bout-time you got here," a red-faced Garth Blackett said stepping off his stoop to meet Clovis in front of his home. Garth was dressed like he always did, dirty jeans, plaid shirt and scuffed work boots. "What're you gonna do about that crazy old fucker who trashed my truck?"

"I've got officers over there getting a statement as we speak," Clovis stated calmly in response. "But I want to be clear here, Mr. Blackett. You're telling me you saw Eli Woodman do this? You saw ninety-three-year-old Eli Woodman come here, and spread this trash in and around your truck?"

"You damn right I did," Garth replied. "Saw him with my own eyes. Pulled up in that rust bucket, 72 Dodge Fargo of his." Garth spat on the ground. "I came outside to stop him, but he pointed a shotgun at me. He done gone and lost his damn mind, I tell ya."

Chief Clovis shifted his stance, adjusted his cap and continued to speak calmly.

"So, I want to be sure I get this straight. Old Eli Woodman came here with a load of trash in his old Fargo and spread this garbage," Clovis gestured towards Garth's truck as he spoke. "Spread all this garbage, all inside and around your truck?"

"That's what I said," Garth replied angrily, puffing out his chest.

"So, he brought the trash with him then? In his truck?"

"Yes, dammit!"

"In that case Mr. Blackett, you wouldn't happen to know where this trash came from? I mean, where Mr. Woodman got the trash that he brought here in his truck?"

Garth Blackett, dumbstruck, stood speechless.

It was obvious to Clovis that the reality of what had just happened finally sunk in for Garth.

"Mr. Blackett, Eli Woodman's called me several times about someone dumping trash on his property. You wouldn't happen to know anything about that, now would you?"

"No," Garth replied without hesitation. "I don't know nothing bout-that. But I tell you, that old fool lost his mind, and you better do something about it. Came here waving around a shotgun."

"Listen, Garth. I got three official complaints from Eli saying someone was dumping trash on his property. Trash you say you know nothing about. Now Eli, comes to your house with a load of trash and spreads it all over *your* truck."

"Exactly," Garth replied. "He came here and spread his trash on my truck."

"His trash," Clovis stated as he reached into his back pocket and pulled out the envelope, he had tucked back there. "His trash that he brought which contains this credit card application with whose name on it?"

Clovis held the envelope so Garth could see it but kept

it out of reach.

"I... uh..." Garth muttered.

The Chief pulled the letter back and turned it around. "Garth Blackett," Clovis read. "How did Eli get your mail?" Clovis tucked the envelope back into his pocket. "If I was to look through the trash in your truck, would I find more stuff I can tie to you as well?"

Garth stood speechless, his shoulders sagging slightly, looking deflated.

"So technically," Chief Clovis added. "He was actually just returning your property, wasn't he, Mr. Blackett?"

Clovis could see that Garth knew he was beat when it came to the trash. It was obvious he had in fact been dumping trash on old Eli Woodman's property. Something he had thought he was getting away with until now.

"Ain't my fault the town's garbage trucks don't come up this way no more," Garth replied as if to justify his dumping trash on someone else's property.

"Did you take it up with the town council?"

"No, but Darla did," Garth said, referring to his neighbor who lived a half mile farther away. "She even called the mayor."

"And what did Jack Ledger have to say about the matter?" Clovis replied, referring to the recently reelected mayor.

Garth snorted and spat before continuing.

"He says it costs the town too much money to come all the way out here for three houses."

"He's right," Clovis replied. "The contract changed hands, and the new crew were going to charge more if they had to do the far outskirts of town."

"How's that my problem?" Garth retorted.

"It is expensive to send the garbage trucks all the way out here for three houses, but you know that already."

"I pay my taxes," Garth blurted confidently, as if that should resolve everything.

"Listen, it was either that or raise your taxes to help pay for it."

"No way," Garth replied angrily. "I pay enough taxes as it is."

"You see, Mr. Blackett," Clovis said with a more serious tone, trying to convey authority without sounding arrogant. "The way the city saw it, you all go to town every other day so they asked that you bring your trash, and they would let you dump it into the dumpster, out behind city hall. This way they won't have to raise anyone's taxes."

"But that costs me money in fuel."

"You already need to get your mail at the town's post office," Clovis stated, thinking that might sway the conversation. "And you drive by the town hall every time you go to Burnett's Place," Clovis added, knowing full well that explaining this part to Garth was pointless.

Everyone knew that Garth Blackett was a regular at the local watering hole. After the gruesome murders there seven years ago most people had assumed the place would have closed for good. Some had hoped it would; who would ever want to go there again? But Jack Ledger bought the place, gutted it, much like the people whose blood had stained the hardwood, and renovated it enough to make it unrecognizable, giving it a new life.

Garth looked defeated but angry still.

"You're not gonna do anything about the trash, are ya?" Garth asked.

"It's yours, isn't it?" Clovis replied, trying hard to stifle a smirk.

"You gonna do something about that shotgun of his?" Garth asked, referring to Eli Woodman brandishing his Winchester.

"What shotgun?" Clovis asked.

Garth's face reddened further. "You know damned well that old fool had a shotgun."

"Tell me, Mr. Blackett. If he didn't have it, what would you have done? Would you have struck him?"

"That old fool deserved an ass-kickin."

"A half blind ninety-three-year-old man?" Clovis said inquisitively, knowing full well what would have happened if Eli hadn't brought his Winchester. Garth Blackett was known to have a temper. It was the reason why his wife left him, after all. He knew this because he had come calling, whenever Garth got riled up and his wife got scared and called the police.

Clovis could tell Garth knew better than to reply to that. What could he say? Garth's downfall was being too proud to let an old man get the better of him and too stubborn to let it go. This was Garth in a nutshell, Clovis thought.

His first instinct would have probably been to drive over to Eli's but what then, thought Clovis. Had Eli not been ninety-three, Garth might have tried to knock his block off anyway. Which made Clovis wonder if old Eli would have pulled that trigger and then they'd have found out the hard way, what that shotgun was loaded with.

"Look, Mr. Blackett. I've got officers at the Woodman residence as we speak making sure nothing like this ever happens again."

"You better," Garth replied while puffing up his chest again as if he wasn't to blame for any of this.

"But Mr. Blackett, if you try and dump trash on Eli's property again, I can't promise he won't shoot you next time."

"You threatening to let the old man shoot me?" Garth asked while glancing at the flies buzzing around the garbage in his truck.

"I'm just saying that now he knows for sure it's you who's been dumping trash on his property and so I'd suggest taking it over to town hall and using those dumpsters, like they asked you to. It's that or your taxes go up."

"It ain't fair, you know."

"I don't make the rules, Garth. Town Council does. But it's my job to keep the peace, which means I need you to quit dumping your trash on old Eli Woodman's property," Clovis said in a firm tone he thought might get the point across. "And to answer your question, no. I'm not going to do anything about it. He was simply returning your property. Besides, if I make this official," Clovis said gesturing towards the vandalized truck. "I'll have to make my findings for Eli's report official about the trash being dumped on his property. A file which by the way, is on my desk as we speak."

Garth Blackett cast his gaze at an empty can of beans at his feet. He kicked the can into the pile of trash and avoided eye contact.

"Are we good?" Chief Clovis asked, wanting to brush this off and not waste time on the mountain of paperwork that would be as useful as the trash pile before him. He had better things to worry about.

"Yeah," Garth replied as he stormed off, went inside and slammed the door behind him.

Clovis limped back to his cruiser while thinking how he wanted to avoid charging someone like Eli Woodman, an old codger that would garner much sympathy around town. But now he wondered how it had gone for Libby and Reggie at the old man's house.

2

AT ABOUT THE SAME time Garth had come out to greet Chief Clovis; Officer Libby Terwilliger had been the one to knock on Eli Woodman's door. She figured Eli would be less rattled if she knocked instead of Officer Keirstead.

Office Keirstead—everyone called him by his first name of Reggie—was an imposing figure. A broad shouldered man who loomed over most while sitting, stood six-foot-six. Libby had met football players who were less imposing and for this reason, Libby figured it best if she did the talking. It wouldn't do to make old Eli feel threatened and do something stupid like pull out his shotgun.

Eli Woodman lived in a dilapidated two-story house, with old white distressed clapboard siding. The roof was in great disrepair and the old red brick chimney looked like the next strong wind might blow it over.

Reggie shifted his footing, and Libby could feel his considerable weight bearing down onto the old wood of the deck, making it sag and creak.

She straightened her shirt, pulled her blond ponytail taut and raised her fist, about to knock on the screen door when the interior door creaked slightly ajar. She took a step back as she heard shuffling feet from behind the doors.

"Mr. Woodman. We're Carlton Police and we'd like to talk to you."

Libby heard old Eli speak from somewhere inside the house.

"I told Clovis someone was dumping garbage on my property. He told me he'd look into it."

"Mr. Woodman, may we come in?" Libby said as she opened the screen door and gently pushed the interior door open.

"Door's open, ain't it?" Libby heard Eli say firmly.

Her right hand resting on her belt near her gun and Taser, Officer Libby stepped inside, assessing the threat level as she did. Eli wasn't in the living room, but she could hear his feet shuffling on the floor from beyond the archway which led into the kitchen. The natural light coming in through the dirty windows illuminated the dust in the air more than the room itself. The dirty old couch had stacked books under its right front corner instead of a wooden leg. The old wood coffee table had multiple rings on it from paint cans mixed in with the stains making it obvious old Eli had never owned coasters. On the wall, above the couch, hung a four-slot gun rack with a single old shotgun in it. Libby felt herself relax slightly at the sight of the racked weapon. She glanced behind her and saw Reggie filling the doorway, nearly blocking as much light as the door would, had it been shut.

"I told Clovis to find that som-bitch who was dumpin trash on my property."

Eli dragged his feet as he stepped into the archway. He wore battered old black shoes, dirty dark slacks, held up by suspenders over an old sweat stained tank top that used to be white, back when it was new. What was left of his wispy white hair was sticking up in every which way, matching his long white eyebrows protruding from his face.

Libby noticed the old man's left eye seemed substantially glazed over, while his right wasn't nearly as bad. Cataracts, she thought. She looked Eli over, noticing his bony shoulders and slouching posture, as if his pelvic bone was thrust forward and the rest of him leaned slightly backwards. In his right hand he held an old, battered tin cup while his other hand was empty, dangling at his side. Libby relaxed a bit more while wondering what was in the old man's cup. She couldn't help but think the old man stood as if all was perfectly normal, as he took a sip from the old, battered tin cup.

"It's that Blackett fella, from up the road. I seen him do it. Dump his trash on my property."

Libby spoke calmly yet with authority. "Mr. Woodman, Chief McPhee is over there as we speak, taking care of the situation."

Libby could feel Reggie's presence behind her as she continued.

"You need to leave it to us. Is that understood?" Libby stated, trying her best not to sound condescending to the ninety-three-year-old. "And you know we're going to have to take that," Libby said glancing at the shotgun on the gun rack.

"It don't work," Eli responded.

Libby glanced over her shoulder at Reggie who was waiting on a cue from the senior officer to collect the shotgun. He stepped over to the couch and plucked the shotgun off the rack, took a step back and stood next to Libby.

"Bought that from a Sears catalogue in 1976," Eli muttered with another sip from his tin cup.

Libby saw Reggie examining the gun. It was in terrible condition. At a glance, she wasn't sure if it could be fired at all as the trigger seemed bent, probably making it impossible to be pulled back. The ejector port looked rusted shut and the barrel seemed bent. Reggie would later tell Libby as they discussed if Sears actually had sold guns in their catalogues back in those days that this gun hadn't been fired in a very long time.

"If you want it back," Libby said, referring to the shotgun Reggie held at his side. "You'll have to talk to Chief McPhee."

Eli Woodman calmly sipped from his tin cup before speaking. "You gonna arrest me?"

"For what?" Libby replied. "As far as the chief is concerned, you were returning Mr. Blackett's property. Weren't you?"

"Yup," Eli replied from behind his tin cup.

"But next time something like this happens, you call us, okay?" Libby added.

Satisfied that old Eli Woodman was calm and that he wouldn't do anything crazy, Officer Libby decided all was fine. She turned sideways, so that Officer Reggie would take her cue to leave as she sidestepped towards the door without taking her eyes off Eli. Libby had seen too much carnage in her career to take chances, even with someone like ninety-three-year-old Eli Woodman. Since the Burnett incident seven years ago, she would never underestimate anyone again.

Reggie stepped off the creaking deck and marched towards the cruiser. He glanced back at Libby who was directly behind him as he spoke.

"I was worried the old man would be ready for a shootout or something."

Libby grinned as she got in the cruiser.

Reggie popped open the trunk to store Eli's old shotgun. As he closed the trunk he turned, as if something caught his eye.

"Who's that?" Reggie asked as he got in the driver's side. Libby saw a car approaching on this rarely travelled road.

"That would be Ernie Woodman. Eli's son." Libby

replied. "Probably delivering groceries."

"Ernie who owns the grocery store is Eli's son?" Reggie asked as he started the cruiser and put it in gear.

"That he is," Libby replied as they drove past Ernie's car on their way back into town. "All the Woodman in the area are related in some way. But Ernie doesn't own the grocery store, he manages it."

"So anyway. Like I was saying before we came out here. You really need to try red wine. I'll recommend a few kinds to try," Reggie said.

"Hold that thought," Libby said as she scooped up the radio and spoke into the mike.

"Chief, you there? Copy?"

3

"*Was that Libby and* Reggie just now?" Ernie Woodman asked as he entered the house where he had been raised. It was more dilapidated now than it had been when he'd grown up here. The floor creaked as he carried a couple of paper grocery bags into the kitchen.

"Yup," Eli muttered in response as he shuffled his feet, walking back from the bathroom into the kitchen and sitting down at his old, white-marbled Formica kitchen table.

"What did they want?" Ernie inquired as he set the grocery bags on the kitchen counter. As he did so, he noticed something out of place. Leaning against the fridge was his father's good Winchester. The same one Ernie had bought him, about twenty Christmases ago. Chalking it up to his father's hate for raccoons in his old woodshed, Ernie picked up the shotgun and took it to the living room to put it back where it belonged.

"They came about the trash on my property," Eli replied. "You bring me any of those little cakes I like?"

"Two boxes," Ernie replied as he racked the shotgun. "Where's your old Winchester? The one you ran over with the Fargo that time that momma bear chased you."

"You bring me eggs?" Eli asked.

Ernie didn't know if his father was ignoring the question about his old shotgun or simply hadn't heard him. Both were possible with Eli.

"Of course, pop," Ernie replied as he reentered the kitchen and started to unpack the groceries. He glanced at his aging father who was hunched over more than usual while sitting at the kitchen table, his favorite tin cup before him.

"What're you drinking?" Ernie asked, knowing full well his father was sipping his favorite rum coffee. He could smell it. It was probably more rum than coffee, he thought.

"Dr. Williams said you should cut back on the coffee," Ernie said, leaving out the part about the rum. "You'll end up with heart palpitations again."

"I'm too old to quit."

"He didn't say to quit," Ernie replied. As a matter of fact, in private Doctor William had told Ernie the opposite. That quitting now, at his age would probably be a shock to his system and might do more harm than good. "Doc said to cut down. Because you were complaining of pain when you pee. That and heart palpitations."

"How's the wife?" Eli asked, clearly changing the subject which Ernie always let his pop do instead of getting him all riled up.

4

POLICE CHIEF CLOVIS MCPHEE sat in his cruiser, parked on the roadside of Pleasant Ridge, on the outskirts of Carlton. The envelope he'd taken from the trash in Garth Blackett's truck was sitting on the passenger seat as Clovis fiddled with his new android phone, wishing he'd have thought to take a picture of Garth's truck covered in garbage. He planned on letting this slide, for both Garth and Eli, if they complied with his simple requests of not dumping any more trash on each other's property. But when the idea crossed his mind that he should have taken a picture of the truck, he remembered that there was something else he wanted a picture of. Something that had been bothering him for years. Something he had been after the town council and the mayor about ever since it was first discovered.

He fiddled with his phone and almost dropped it when the screen lit up brightly, displaying an incoming call. He swallowed hard when he saw the caller display and quickly answered the call from his wife.

"Hey," Clovis said. "Is everything okay?"

"Yeah, everything's fine," Raylene replied. "I just wanted to hear your voice."

"You sure everything's okay?"

"Yeah," she replied. "Is this a bad time?"

"Not at all."

"Where are you?"

"Out in Pleasant Ridge," Clovis replied.

"Did they fix it yet?" Raylene inquired.

She knew where he would be without asking, Clovis thought.

"Not yet."

"You need to let that go," Raylene said. "You've got bigger fish to fry."

"I know," Clovis replied. "But I wanted to get a picture of it, now that I have this fancy new phone you got me."

Clovis regretted saying that as soon as the words came out of his mouth. Raylene had had good reason to want to get him a new phone, but he didn't want to dwell on that. Not yet anyway.

"It does take amazing pictures for a phone," Raylene replied cheerfully.

Clovis heard the deflection in her tone of voice. His wife clearly didn't want to talk about the reason she gifted him the new phone either.

"I was trying to figure out how to save the picture," Clovis replied.

"Did you take one?" Raylene asked.

"Yes, I did."

"You don't have to save it. The phone does that automatically."

"Really?"

"Yes, silly," Raylene said with humor in her voice.

Clovis smiled. It felt good to hear happiness in his wife's voice again. He felt his emotions well up inside him as he cleared his throat and spoke.

"I need to send this picture to slacker Jack."

"Stop that," Raylene replied firmly. "I hate it when you trash talk Jack Ledger."

"Sorry," Clovis replied.

"I know you want it fixed. I mean you even raised the money to do it."

"It's a matter of principle, at this point. And Jack said the town council was afraid people would be upset if they fixed it. He said we should wait a while. I mean it's been six years, Raylene. How much longer does he want to wait?"

"Come home," Raylene replied. "Just for a bit. I'll make coffee and we can sit a little while before you go back to work."

"I'll be there soon," Clovis replied. "Love you," he added as they ended the call.

He pulled the phone away from his ear and sure enough, the picture he had taken was still there. Although now icons were on top of the picture. He lifted his cap, scratched his head wondering how he had done this. He had set the picture as a background, and he had no idea how. He looked up at the sign before him and then back at the picture on the phone. It was still there, he thought. Raylene would know how to fix it, he told himself. She was better at gadgets than he.

He set the phone down in the passenger seat and started his cruiser but stared at the sign before him.

Welcome to Carlton

Someone had spray painted *Population 1236* on the decorative wooden sign, then painted a line across the number and replaced it with *1232*, written in the same black paint.

A year after the Burnett killings, someone had commemorated the anniversary by defacing the sign, subtracting the number of the dead from the town's population. Clovis had been okay with leaving it as is at first, as a sober reminder of the stupidity of the person who had done the vandalizing. He thought that once they caught the perpetrator that having displayed his insensitivity would be an added shame above whatever the law could throw at them. But now, six years later, they had never caught the perp, and he wanted the sign changed. It was time, he thought as he drove off, heading home for coffee with his schoolteacher wife who was off for the summer. Quick trips like that had become habit since she had been off. Considering the circumstances they now faced, he knew nobody at the station would dare say anything about it. Although Officer Dwayne Adams from the graveyard shift would tease him about the new fancy phone when he found out about it. Clovis and Raylene would share a laugh about this over coffee.

Part 2

Foolish Pride

5

CHIEF CLOVIS MCPHEE STOOD ON the side of Main Street, on a gentle hill in the middle of town, in front of the Saint Francis Catholic Church's newly installed crosswalk. Following the instructions of town council, city workers had installed signs instead of the flashing amber lights Clovis had petitioned for.

"How's Raylene?" Father Finnigan inquired as he strode out of the church, across the concrete area where the hearses parked during funerals and paused to stand next to Clovis.

Clovis knew the father was making small talk instead of getting to the point of his call.

"Good," Clovis answered, leaving out the part about having to leave home faster than he had wanted to, after coffee and sandwiches. Although he would never say it, Clovis was glad the good father had only called after they were done eating.

"I guess this was bound to happen, wasn't it?" Father Finnigan said in an inquisitive tone.

"Jack Ledger's going to be all smiles when he hears about this," Clovis stated.

"Jack? Happy? About this?" the father asked. "Why would the mayor be happy about this?"

"Because he said it would happen."

"Right. I do recall him saying that but that was last

summer," Finnigan replied. "When they added signs and repainted the crosswalk, right after that kid got hit by a car."

"Oh, I remember. Anyway, Jack said it would happen, and it did. Just like he predicted so that'll make him happy."

"I guess you know Jack better than I do then," Father Finnigan replied.

"That I do," Clovis stated with a tone conveying exasperation.

"I suppose he did say this would happen, which is why he voted against it."

"Well, I for one am glad it took a year before someone finally did it," Clovis said as they watched a car slow as it drove past, the driver looking their way.

Clovis felt disappointment over the idea that Jack Ledger was right after all. Right about someone vandalizing the rainbow crosswalk which crossed the street in front of the church. The town council had voted for it, and although most everyone approved it, a few did predict it wouldn't be well received by some. Clovis wanted to believe their community was more open minded than the mayor did.

The rainbow crosswalk, which had been a bold white grid filled with the colors of the rainbow flag had lasted a full year before someone defaced it. Black paint had been poured over it and in a hurry by the looks of it. Large black splotches covering it in parts, spilling over onto the asphalt around it.

"It had to have been done last night," Father Finnigan said. "It wasn't there yesterday. I only noticed it about an hour ago."

"Damn, Jack Ledger's gonna be strutting like a peacock, all proud he was right after all," Clovis muttered, recalling how Jack was back in high school. He had known Jack since then and his stubborn pride was always something he had disliked about him.

"Pardon?" Finnigan asked as if he hadn't understood.

They watched another passing car slow down to look their way, the driver obviously curious as to what was going on as he saw the chief of police with the good father standing by the roadside.

"Nothing," Clovis replied.

"Bonnie's going to love this," Father Finnigan muttered, referring to Bonnie Campbell, owner of the Carlton Gazette.

"She'll be here soon enough," Clovis replied, knowing full well the story would make the front page of the small, struggling weekly newspaper.

"She already has," Father Finnigan replied. "She took a bunch of pictures and left in a hurry before I could speak with her."

Clovis muttered something as he pulled his phone from his pocket and snapped a few pictures of the defaced rainbow crosswalk while Father Finnigan watched. Clovis examined the pictures, wanting to be sure he had properly captured the situation, wondering why he hadn't gotten a phone like this years ago. The camera alone was coming in handy, he thought as he pinched his fingers into the screen and spread them like his wife had shown him, zooming in and carefully examining the scene as if under a magnifying glass. He paused, seeing something in the image that caught his attention. He looked up from the phone and saw that same something in the grass, on the other side of the road.

Limping across the street, Chief Clovis stopped and took another picture before stooping down to carefully pick up a battered, dirty, black paint covered lid from a paint can. He examined it for anything that might indicate where it had come from. He wasn't surprised to find it void of any useful labels or markings of any kind, save dirt and the tool marks of what had to be a screwdriver used to pry the paint can open.

"Is that evidence?" Father Finnigan asked from across the street, startling Clovis who had been lost in the moment.

"Yes," Clovis replied as he made his way across the street to the church parking lot where his cruiser was. "I would think that it is, considering the circumstances." Clovis popped the trunk of his cruiser and tossed the lid casually into it before slamming the trunk shut.

"Have you thought about taking some time off, Clovis?" Father Finnigan inquired.

"And do what?" Clovis replied dryly without making eye contact.

6

Still standing in the church parking lot as they watched another car slowly drive by, Father Finnigan wanted to tell Clovis, go spend time with your wife. Your family. Although he wasn't sure he should. He couldn't recall if the Chief's kids had come home recently. His son Cotton was a soldier off on a peacekeeping mission, last he'd heard. Finnigan didn't want to ask and worry them more than they already were. And the Chief's daughter Anna should be home sometime during the summer, he thought. She had gone to Paris with friends for a month. At least that was the rumor about town.

"Well, if you ever need to talk," Father Finnigan added as Chief Clovis got into his cruiser and drove away.

Father Finnigan pulled his iPhone from his pocket, dialed and put the phone to his ear. The phone barely completed a single ring before being picked up.

"Raylene? It's Father Finnigan." He heard a gasp on the other end of the line before she spoke.

"Father... what's wrong? Is it Clovis?"

"Oh, nothing's wrong, dear. But I have been meaning to call you. To talk. Unless you'd rather not, that is."

"It's okay, Father Finnigan. I understand you mean well. But it feels like talking about it only makes it real. Like if we don't talk about it, it's not really happening."

"I'm sorry, Raylene." Father Finnigan spoke with regret for having called.

"It's okay, Father. How's the Penny Sale coming along?" Raylene asked.

Father Finnigan thought she sounded desperate to change the subject to something she could handle.

7

BONNIE CAMPBELL SAT AT her desk, lost in thought about how she had finally done it. Against the advice of a few close friends, she had made the decision to go through with it. It was time, she had told them. She cancelled her usual appointment, bought the kit and committed herself. She had stopped lying about her white hair. She was so elated when she had finally dyed it completely white instead of silver that she was tempted to do a full-page article on herself in the next edition of The Carlton Gazette. That was the perk of owning the small local paper, doing what you wanted. Sure, it wasn't news, but feel-good articles were what she often did when there was nothing major to write about.

Local woman accepts the fact that she's not getting any younger, the headline would read. She smiled to herself as she opened the desk drawer out of habit. Her smile vanished, realizing what she had just done. She had reached for the bottle she used to keep in the drawer, handy for just such a moment. But Bonnie had quit drinking. She closed the drawer, adjusted her scarf and woke her computer from sleep mode. She closed her eyes and took a deep breath, fighting off the temptation to grab her large handbag and head directly to the liquor store.

Bonnie quit drinking once she'd heard about Clovis and his wife Raylene. When the rumor mill made its way to her, she had been on the tail end of a two-day drunk and had said the most inappropriate things to her secret lover. Something she instantly feared would be revealed, had they not been trying to keep their fling discreet.

Bonnie hadn't had a drink since but craved one now. Desperately. She tried to busy herself so she could get it off her mind. She pulled her digital camera from her large handbag, turned it on and connected it to her computer. She set the images to download to her computer and absentmindedly reached for the drawer a second time. The real withdrawal symptoms not yet taking their toll, she took yet another deep breath.

As the images of the defaced rainbow crosswalk downloaded to her computer, Bonnie refocused and typed up what she thought was a great but simple headline for the front page of this week's edition of The Carlton Gazette.

Rainbow Crosswalk Defaced.

Tight, concise and to the point, she mused as she removed and cleaned her glasses.

She glanced at the phone on her desk, wondering how long it would take for Chief Clovis to call her. He surely would, after what had happened. He would pressure her into not writing a divisive article. The bulk of the townsfolk had been okay with the crosswalk, but there had been grumblings. Some voicing opposition, not hiding their old-fashioned views. Others with concerns about outright bigotry that most knew were unfounded.

"How should I explain this to my six-year-old?" a father had asked at an open town council meeting.

"By explaining bigotry," Chief Clovis had replied in front of the town council and everyone in attendance.

Bonnie had liked that.

She adjusted herself, sitting upright and began writing this article in a way she hadn't thought possible.

Sober.

"Mayor Jack Ledger's prediction came true as the church's rainbow crosswalk was targeted by bigots," wrote Bonnie. She sat back and pondered if she liked this turn of phrase or not. Something she never used to do when she was drunk. While intoxicated, she cared much less about how it read but worried solely about selling ads and making money. Now she found herself worried about the writing. Something she hadn't done in a long time.

8

Libby sat in her Jeep, takeout cardboard coffee cup in hand as she stared at the quiet police station before her. Casting long morning shadows were the trio of police cruisers neatly lined up in front of the building. She sipped coffee and glanced at the time.

Chief Clovis was late again. This had been happening so much that he had suggested that Libby stop picking up coffee for him on her way to work. Instead, he would have one at home. That would give him more time with Raylene since she was off for the summer, he had added to justify his request.

With this on her mind, Libby exited her Jeep and went inside to find Officer Dwayne Adams in his usual position. His chair leaning back with his feet up on the desk, his chin almost resting on his chest, snoring away. He even had his customary spot of drool on his shirt, this time, just above the breast pocket. On the desk was a battered copy of *Wayward* by Blake Crouch, the second book from a series that Dwayne kept raving about.

Libby quietly made her way into the police bullpen, being careful not to wake Dwayne. She eased herself into her chair, sipped coffee as she gently jiggled her mouse and woke her computer.

Avoid spoilers, read the first book from the trilogy called *Pines*, she recalled him insisting.

Dwayne stirred, snorted and began snoring again.

Libby watched him sleep, recalling all the times she and Chief Clovis found Dwayne in just such a situation. She smiled at the memory of Clovis making sudden noises to startle Dwayne awake, sometimes making him topple his chair over and sprawling on the floor. When this happened, he'd comically scramble to get up and compose himself. Libby smiled at the memory of the time Clovis used an air horn to rouse Dwayne. Or the time he and Libby set all the clocks in the station ahead by four hours and pretended Dwayne had slept half the day.

"Your wife called," Clovis had told Dwayne. "We told her you'd run off with another woman," Clovis had lied.

Libby felt herself becoming emotional as she recalled the memories of happier times. She palmed away a tear and sipped coffee as she heard Dwayne shuffle in his chair.

"What time is it?" Dwayne asked yawning wide as he stretched out the kinks caused by his bizarre napping ritual.

"Time for you to go home to your wife," Libby replied.

Dwayne took his feet off the desk, accidentally knocking his book to the floor in the process.

"Is Clovis in yet?" he asked as he stood, twisting and stretching, his joints popping and crackling loud enough for Libby to hear, making her stomach churn.

"Stop that," Libby said.

Dwayne knew full well that bothered her but did it anyway.

"And no, Clovis isn't in yet."

"I was going to ask him about the crosswalk."

"The what?"

"The crosswalk. You know... the rainbow crosswalk in front of the church."

"What about it?" Libby asked as she leaned back, put her feet up on her desk and sipped coffee.

"You didn't hear? Someone poured black paint all over the crosswalk."

Dwayne fetched his ball cap from the coat hooks on the back wall, put it on and patted his pockets as if looking for something.

"You serious?" Libby asked while pointing to what she assumed Dwayne was searching for, his keys under the papers on his desk.

"Yup," Dwayne said scooping up his keys.

"Damn... I wonder if Jack knows about this?"

Libby sat up, opened Facebook and logged in and just as she suspected, the first post she saw was about the act of vandalism.

"The whole town probably knows by now, except you

of course," Dwayne quipped.

"I gotta tell Clovis about this."

Dwayne, keys in hand, flopped into his desk chair and spun to face Libby.

"Clovis? He knows. Word is, Father Finnigan called him after he saw Bonnie Campbell snooping around. That's when he saw it and called the chief."

"That's strange… he never said anything to you about this?" Libby asked.

"Nope. And according to Father Finnigan, the chief took some pictures and even found a lid from a paint can."

"Get out-a-town! You serious?"

"Yup. Father Finnigan said the chief tossed it into the trunk of his car and left."

"I'm sure he had good reason," Libby replied, thinking about how he had told them to *not* put the Woodman trash incident on the books. How he had wanted to handle it himself. She couldn't help but wonder if maybe he felt the same about the crosswalk.

"Jack Ledger and his foolish pride is gonna love this one," Dwayne said while fingering his keys.

"Why would you say that?"

"He predicted this very thing would happen."

"True. I do remember something about that."

"Didn't Jack vote against the rainbow crosswalk?"

"Nope. Some say he did but that's not true. He voted to allow it. Said he didn't really care if they put one up or not. He said something like, I don't believe in telling others how to live their lives."

"That's noble… sorta."

"Yeah, but he did predict some people wouldn't like it. Something about the older members of the church perhaps not understanding. And he predicted some closed-minded bigot would do something just like this."

"Well turns out he was right," Libby said as she scrolled down her Facebook feed and began reading the comments on a post about the vandalism.

"Well Maureen must be home by now," Dwayne said.

His wife worked the graveyard shift at Sleepy Meadows.

"Go home, Dwayne," Libby replied. "Tell Maureen I said hi."

Part 3

Christmas in July

9

THE SETTING SUN NOW HIDDEN behind the row of houses at their backs, Jack Ledger and Clovis McPhee leaned onto the side of the Chief's police cruiser. The police car sat directly behind the mayor's silver sedan. Side by side, the men leaned casually, arms crossed looking at the scene before them.

"I told Libby not to bother you with this," the mayor said to Clovis.

"She knows better than to not tell me," Clovis replied dryly.

"It's just… you know. And I mean, it's not like this is a big deal but the few tourists that do come through town will wonder what kind of town we have here. I mean it's the middle of summer, for Pete's sake," Jack muttered. "I've heard of Christmas in July but give me a break."

"I see," Clovis replied as they marveled at the house before them.

The modest home, nestled in the middle of the little town, was heavily decorated with Christmas paraphernalia. The decorations had remained up since the previous holiday season and had been lit every day since early May.

"She added a new one," Jack said, sighing as he spoke. "Last night. She bought it through Amazon, I'm told." Jack pointed to an animated Santa Claus, whose arm raised every so often as he drank from a vintage 7-up bottle.

"You know there's no law against this, right?" Clovis asked.

"We're going to discuss it at the next council meeting."

"She cuts her lawn," Clovis stated.

"We plan on making it a city ordinance."

"She pays her taxes," Clovis added.

"Where you can decorate your house but only if it fits the season or whatever," Jack replied bitterly, ignoring the Chief's comments.

"It's her electric bill," Clovis quipped, knowing he was getting under the mayor's thin skin.

"A few decorations would be fine," Jack said. "But I mean, this is getting ridiculous." Jack gestured towards the brightly lit house as he said this.

Clovis grinned. A part of him liked it. Especially late at night, when the town was quiet. He and Raylene had recently driven out a few times, when most everyone was sleeping. They had parked nearby, sitting together, basking in the glow of the Christmas lights as they cuddled in his truck. But the Mayor wouldn't understand this. Clovis assumed Jack didn't have a single romantic bone in his body.

"I'll talk to her," Clovis said as he stepped forward, adjusted his baseball cap and turned to face the mayor.

"We're not being unreasonable, you know," Jack stated while glaring at the Chief.

Clovis thought the mayor's statement might be an attempt to justify his contempt for the Christmas decorations.

He watched Jack pull his keys from his pocket and march toward his car.

Clovis marveled at the fact that the mayor had said 'we' and not 'I'. 'We' as in the town council. As if they all unanimously supported the ordinance. Clovis was doubtful about that.

"I said I'll talk to her," Clovis repeated. "But I'm not telling her to take them down. She's not breaking any laws."

"Not yet," Jack replied as he got into his car and drove away.

Clovis watched the mayor drive off before turning to see old Ms. Musgrave standing at her door, smiling at him. He knew she had been watching through the blinds in her living room. He had noticed them moving a little as he chatted with the mayor. As he limped up the sidewalk, the elderly woman who had been great friends with his late mother smiled and opened her screen door. Her smile widened as Clovis approached.

"Come in, come in. How's Raylene?" Ms. Musgrave asked as Clovis entered her home.

"Are those oatmeal cookies I smell?" Clovis asked as he took off his cap.

"Fresh from the oven," Ms. Musgrave replied with a coy smile.

"You knew I was coming."

"Of course. Mayor Ledger drove by last night while I was putting up my new Santa Claus. Do you like it?" Ms. Musgrave asked with a smile as she led Clovis to her kitchen and motioned for him to sit at the table.

"I sure do," Chief Clovis replied as he sat. "My mom had one just like it, although it didn't light up or move or anything. But I remember her hanging it every year."

"Tea?" the elderly woman asked with warmth in her voice.

"I'd love some," Clovis replied.

Ms. Musgrave put a kettle on her stove and placed a plate of cookies on the center of her small kitchen table.

"The mayor sent you to talk to me about my Christmas decorations, I take it?"

Clovis smiled wide as he reached for a warm cookie.

10

An hour later, in Bonnie Campbell's dimly lit bedroom, she got up and found her leopard print top on the floor near the door. It had recently been hastily removed and cast aside without regard.

"You haven't said a thing about my hair," Bonnie stated as she put her blouse back on. "It's like you haven't even noticed."

Bonnie sat on the edge of the bed and looked back at her lover who still lay on the bed, fingers interlaced, hands resting on his round belly.

"I'm sorry," Jack Ledger muttered as he scratched himself through boxer shorts, he had slipped back on moments ago. "I just got a lot on my mind, is all."

"It pains me to admit that you were right about that stupid crosswalk," Bonnie stated as she crawled back onto the bed and lay down beside Jack, resting her head on his shoulder.

Jack put his arm around her as he spoke.

"Actually, it's that old lady Musgrave and her damned Christmas decorations. I mean its July, for Pete's sake."

"I think it's sweet," Bonnie replied.

"What? Her decorations? Sweet?" Jack asked incredulously.

In that moment, Bonnie lifted her head off her lover's shoulder as she realized that he was oblivious to why Ms. Musgrave still had her Christmas decorations up. She couldn't believe that the one and only Jack Ledger, the mayor who prided himself on always being up to speed with the goings-on in *his* little town, didn't know why sweet little old Ms. Musgrave hadn't taken down her decorations yet. He didn't have a clue as to why she had started lighting them again, even if the holidays were so far away.

But she couldn't help but be irritated that he had been right after all about the crosswalk. Although he had predicted actual outrage which hadn't panned out so at least there was that. But the vandalism had the mayor strutting around like a peacock, with his I told you so smug grin that very afternoon the vandalism had been discovered.

"Sweet?" Jack said bitterly after a long pause. "Are you on the sauce again?" he said as he pulled away and sat on the edge of the bed.

"Go poke that dick of yours in a blender, you ass," Bonnie replied coldly. She hadn't even told Jack that she was trying to quit drinking. Jack wasn't the type to notice the little things, or even the big things like her hair or the fact that she had a real drinking problem. When Jack had arrived, she had had white hair instead of the boxed silver she had been for the last ten years. But Jack had been too busy obsessing over the stupid Christmas decorations to notice. All he had wanted was to get his rocks off, and now that he had done just that, he was back to stressing over the decorations.

But Bonnie knew the real reason he was so upset. It was no secret that when he had politely asked Ms. Musgrave to take them down, she had told him to get off her property or she would call Chief McPhee and have him removed. This had hurt his pride more than anything else. Ms. Musgrave, who was normally so nice to everyone, had been quite cold to the mayor, as if she had taken great offense to his request.

Jack picked up his pants off the floor, lifted a leg, staggered and almost fell over while putting them on.

Bonnie turned her back to Jack and finished getting dressed.

"You write that article about the crosswalk?" Jack inquired, glancing over his shoulder at his lover.

Bonnie heard some of the smug pride return in the mayor's voice when he spoke. She couldn't lie and say no. He'd know. There wasn't a lot going on in town and so there wasn't much to write about. This was a juicy story and they both knew it. Plus, many people would actually want to know what Bonnie had to say about this. She would give them both the facts and her point of view as well. That was what she did.

"It's not finished yet," Bonnie replied.

"Don't you go to press today?"

Bonnie knew Jack was confused as he assumed she should have sent the paper to the printing press by now.

Jack had never actually caught up to the times and didn't realize that all that took less time than it used to. This week's paper was almost ready and so a few minutes behind the computer and the latest edition would be sent to the printer.

"Don't worry about that," Bonnie said as she walked out of her bedroom and left home, leaving Jack behind to finish getting dressed.

It was late but if she kept talking to Jack, he would drive her to drink. This was something she desperately wanted to avoid so she found herself headed to the office to simply get away from the smugness of Jack Ledger, mayor and know-it-all. He had a key after all so could lock up on his way out. Plus, she wouldn't give him the satisfaction of knowing he was right about her needing to finish the paper. Obsessing over the writing had almost made her late to go to print. Almost, she thought as she drove to the rented office space she could no longer afford.

11

Jack Ledger sat behind the wheel of his sedan, marveling at the irritating glow of Ms. Musgrave's Christmas lights. If this had been December, he'd proudly enjoy them like everyone else, but it wasn't. It was July and Jack could feel his blood pressure rise at the mere sight before him.

Pulling his cellphone from his pocket, he made a call.

"Clovis, did I wake you?" Jack asked cringing as he noticed the time. The clock in the dashboard read 11:33.

"Nope," Jack heard Clovis reply. "Couldn't sleep."

"What's this I hear about Eli Woodman, brandishing a shotgun while at the Blackett house?"

Jack heard Clovis sigh.

"People at the bar are talking," Jack said, leaving out the part about Bonnie Campbell not being aware of this yet. He should know as he had been there before going to the bar and she certainly would have told him about this had she known.

"And here I was, thinking you were calling me to tell me you were finally getting the town limit sign fixed," Clovis replied.

Jack gritted his teeth and rolled his eyes. Clovis simply wouldn't let that go, so best to change the subject, he thought.

"Is it true?" Jack asked, repeating something he had heard at Burnett's Place a half-hour ago. "That he had a shotgun? That he threatened Garth?"

"Had… had a shotgun," Clovis replied. "Libby and Reggie took it from him."

"Can they do that?" Jack asked.

"They did. On my orders."

"Ah. I heard that Eli lost his mind or something."

"Don't believe everything you hear, Jack."

"But you just said you took the old coot's shotgun?"

Jack heard Clovis sigh again and knew he shouldn't have called Eli an old coot, even if he felt it was true. He heard rumblings. It sounded as if Clovis's wife Raylene was saying something.

"I took care of it," Clovis replied with an air of impatience.

"Why would Eli pull a gun?" Jack asked as if he deserved an answer.

"I said I took care of it, Jack."

Jack watched as the ornamental Santa Clause on the front of Ms. Musgrave's house raised his arm and fake drink from a vintage 7-up bottle.

"You know I need to know these things, Clovis!" Jack replied, in a very matter of fact tone.

"No, you don't, Jack. You're the mayor and *I'm* the chief of police. It's my job to keep the peace, not yours."

"Sorry," Jack muttered, knowing full well he shouldn't be pissing Clovis off in his current situation.

"Just drop it," Clovis replied in calm tone of voice. "And get that stupid sign fixed."

Jack could hear Raylene saying something as the call ended. He looked at his phone to be certain, plopped it onto the passenger seat and turned his attention to the Christmas decorations up the street.

"Dammit," he muttered, wondering what to do. The city council hadn't yet officially discussed his idea of the proposed bylaw, but from some of his conversations with the other council members, he knew it wouldn't go his way. Most of them opposed the idea of telling the citizens of Carlton what they could and couldn't put up for decorations, no matter what time of year it was. But it was July, and he was the mayor, so he felt he should be able to have a say in the matter.

Jack sighed in frustration, started his car and drove by the house slowly, thinking about ways he could maybe sabotage some of the lights. He had to do something, he thought.

12

Ms. Musgrave peeked through the blinds in the window of her front door as she watched Mayor Jack Ledger's car drive slowly past her brightly lit house. She had been making her way back to bed when something on the floor had caught her eye. An envelope in front of her door. It had clearly been slipped through her mail slot.

She smiled through the pain in her hip, bending to pick it up.

This wasn't the first time this had happened. Someone had slipped an envelope through her mail slot. She assumed it was someone from her neighborhood but had no way of knowing for sure who it could be. The envelopes were always blank, the contents always anonymous and dropped off at night so as to not to be seen. An obvious attempt to remain anonymous. But since the envelope wasn't there moments before, she peeked through her blinds, in hopes of perhaps catching a glimpse of the persons responsible for it and instead saw the Mayor's car slowly drive past her home.

She knew Jack wouldn't be the one who had snuck it in

her mail slot. The mayor made no secret of the fact that he hated that she still had her Christmas lights up. She wondered if Jack had seen who dropped it off as she opened the envelope and counted the money inside it.

Seventy-five dollars in small bills.

The person or persons didn't even bother with a note this time. Only the first few of the envelopes had a note, saying it was to help with the cost of the electricity to keep her Christmas decorations lit. Only the envelopes always added up to more than the bill itself, so Ms. Musgrave had used the leftover funds to purchase a few more decorations. With this new contribution, she would have enough to get that inflatable Christmas tree with the elves for her lawn. She smiled at the thought of how much that would irritate Jack Ledger as she turned and made her way back to bed. Who would have thought Christmas lights in July would turn out to be so much fun. But with the real reason for the decorations on her mind, she palmed away a tear but smiled still at the thought of it getting under Jack's skin.

Part 4

News to Me

13

STANDING IN THE MORNING SUN at the end of his cobblestone driveway, Jack Ledger picked up the bundle that was the local paper. He pulled the newspaper out of the plastic sleeve it shared with the local flyers and tucked the flyers under his arm. He held up the paper and read the bold large print headline, wondering what his lover Bonnie Campbell would have to say.

Rainbow Crosswalk Defaced

Having caught a glimpse of his name just below the headline, Jack glanced up and down his street to see if anybody was watching. He felt a sudden pang of paranoia as he refocused on the paper and kept reading.

Mayor Jack Ledger's prediction came true as the rainbow crosswalk in front of the church was targeted by bigots.

Jack frowned. He wasn't sure how he felt about this. Why would Bonnie feel the need to make this about him, he wondered. Why wouldn't she focus on what happened instead? He knew darned well she would make what she called an 'act of vandalism' front page news. There was nothing else going on worthy of the front page in the small-town newspaper. What else could she write about? Christmas decorations in July? The rumors of Eli's clash with Garth Blackett were just rumors to most and Clovis wouldn't confirm or deny it, even to the mayor. There was no reason to believe that he would have said anything to Bonnie Campbell. The crosswalk being defaced was the obvious choice for front page news. But why start the article referencing what he had predicted?

Was Bonnie still upset about his not commenting on her new hairstyle? Truthfully, he had thought it suited her very nicely. She looked lovely. But the white reminded him how old they both were, and he didn't like that part. The white hair was a reminder of the pills he now had to take so that he could still be virile enough to have this fling he and Bonnie started a year ago.

At the time, they had been arguing about the old archives of the Carlton Gazette. The local newspaper that he used to own and had to sell once he had gotten elected as mayor, due to the conflict of interest. And Bonnie Campbell, who had purchased the paper, had assumed that its archives would be properly catalogued and readily available. She had assumed wrong.

After years of nagging the mayor, she finally learned that while he had kept an archive of newspapers, they were in print form only. Jack had multiple copies of every paper he ever published, stored in boxes in one of his warehouses, on the backlot of one of his apartment buildings. Getting them from him was something that almost became a legal battle, until he conceded that he hadn't excluded the archives from the sale of the newspaper. And since the only archive he had was in print form, he had no choice but to give her access to them. Something that eventually led to them spending a lot of late hours together, in the backlot warehouse. Which eventually led to a few drinks, which led to their first awkward sexual encounter in a backroom that had an old foldout couch.

Jack realized he was still standing in his driveway, paper in hand, daydreaming of Bonnie and the first time they had sex. Filled with a sudden sense of dread, he folded the paper, glanced at his neighbors' homes to see if they were watching as he made his way inside to finish reading the article.

14

Standing in the dimly lit McPhee kitchen, Raylene poured coffee into a pair of coffee mugs that read HERS and HERS TOO as she spoke.

"Did Bonnie tell you she was thinking of making the paper an online paper only?"

"What?" Clovis asked, looking up from his copy of the Carlton Gazette.

"Bonnie," Raylene continued. "She told me she was thinking of making the Gazette an online paper only."

"Why would she do a thing like that?" Clovis asked as he folded the small newspaper and watched his wife set the coffee mugs on the kitchen table.

"Lower operating costs, easier to sell digital ads than print ads, she says."

Clovis grunted in response, set down his paper and pushed his half full plate away from him and reached for his coffee.

"Not hungry?" Raylene asked.

"You made too much," he replied, trying to justify only eating half his breakfast.

"Anyway," Raylene added, changing the subject as she sat at the table and sipped her coffee. "Bonnie has been looking at doing the paper online only, but the printing company gave her a price break so that she keeps printing. They make money off the flyers they make but are afraid the locals won't want the bundle tossed in their driveways without the local paper included."

"I wonder what Jack Ledger thinks of that."

"I don't think Bonnie told him yet."

"I wonder what he'll think when she does," Clovis wondered aloud as he scooped up the paper again and began reading the front-page article again but this time aloud for his wife to hear.

Raylene palmed away a tear. She sipped her coffee and listened to the love of her life read the cover story of the paper. Something he did when he wanted to know what she thought about the subject at hand.

15

THE SANTORENE DINER AND coffee shop had been retrofitted long ago to look more like it had in the fifties. Most of the older patrons ate there for the sense of nostalgia they got out of the dining experience, reminiscing about days gone by. Most of the younger residents of the small community ate there because the food was fantastic and the coffee even better. The coffee was so good that at ten in the morning the lineup for said coffee, taken to go, was constant.

Mick Miller, owner-operator of the struggling local comic shop was standing behind Ernie Woodman who had just placed his coffee order.

Miller was a man Ernie Woodman had a hard time taking seriously as he sold comic books for a living.

"Did you guys read today's paper?" Mick asked aloud to all who were listening.

Still at the counter, waiting on his order, Ernie turned to look at Mick. As the manager of the local grocery store, Ernie didn't like to be viewed as one to partake in gossip, let alone be the one to spread it but sometimes he couldn't help himself.

"Yes. I did. And while I'm not surprised it finally happened, I'm not sure why it made the front page of the paper. Why glorify stupidity?" Ernie asked.

16

LAST IN THE SANTORENE coffee lineup, was Garth Blackett who snorted in reply, muffling his amusement at the conversation he thought was getting dumber and dumber by the minute. Garth was normally not the type to stay quiet about something he thought was stupid like advertising his town tolerated queers, as he so eloquently would have put it. But Garth was standing in line behind Officer Libby who he didn't want to give reason to notice him any more than necessary. Garth hated cops.

17

"I THINK IT'S A conversation that needs to be had," Libby stated to everyone in the diner. She supported the idea of acknowledging that the small community accepted everyone. Lord knows she had felt discriminated against on numerous occasions because people suspected her to be gay, even though she wasn't. Being a tomboy and a cop did make people question her sexuality, even though it was none of their business. Except Officer Reggie. She couldn't help thinking she wouldn't mind making her sexuality Reggie's business. Libby snapped back to reality as she continued.

"I think whoever did it needs to be outed for it," Libby added.

"That's rich," Garth muttered.

Libby had thought it odd that he hadn't voiced an opinion yet but clearly Garth could no longer keep quiet on the matter.

"Actually, I agree," Mick stated. "I think it's a good thing to know who the intolerant shit is."

"I'm hoping it was a random act and not deliberate," Libby stated as they watched Ernie leave with his coffee.

"Gotta get back to work," Ernie mumbled as he exited the Santorene.

Mick placed his order before turning back towards Libby.

"I agree with what you said earlier. I think the persons responsible need to be outed as the bigots they are," Mick said.

Garth grunted and walked away from the line and headed for the bathroom.

18

As Garth pushed a small shopping cart down the aisle of Ernie Woodman's grocery store, he ruminated about recent events. Garth has always been the type to dwell on things, especially if they upset him. Like not speaking his opinion in the coffee shop about that stupid rainbow crosswalk would bother him all morning, perhaps longer, running the conversation through his mind, over and over. Although not as much as last Friday's incident when he showed up late for work which led to an argument with the site foreman. Garth knew he would have to bite the bullet on this one and it pissed him off. He knew he was in the wrong, as he was often late for work. Most often he would only be a few minutes late and he got away with it.

Local heavy equipment operators were rare and so his boss was lenient for the most part. But Friday he had been three hours late and that was unacceptable, according to his boss. So, when he finished the weeklong project of digging one of the new cranberry beds, he was sent home, not to return until next week when the deliveries of clay, sand and gravel would start to arrive. Only then would the boss call him in to start work again, building the new cranberry beds. So, Garth found himself with free time on his hands and that gave him ample opportunity to do what he did best. Dwell on things that bothered him.

With a small shopping cart half full of canned foods, pizza boxes and premade meals, Garth rounded the corner and spotted Ernie Woodman straightening out a six-foot-tall display of toilet paper bundles. The sight of Ernie at that moment brought everything rushing back and Garth blurted out the first thing that came to mind.

"Your old man must have some sort of death wish, coming out to my place like that."

19

Ernie Woodman often took the time to walk through what he thought of as his grocery store to straighten things out. Of course, he had staff for that but sometimes he preferred to do it himself. It felt therapeutic to do so. Putting things in their place and straightening up, taking stock of what needed refilling and ordered. So, he often got lost in the task and this is why he heard someone saying something but hadn't understood what had been said.

"Pardon me?" Ernie muttered as he turned to see Garth Blackett, one his father's few neighbors standing nearby with a shopping cart half full of what he often referred to as bachelor food.

"I said, your father must have a death wish, bringing a shotgun to my house."

"What?" Ernie asked, wondering if he understood what Garth had said just then.

"Your father must think he's some sort of badass."

"I'm sorry. I don't understand what you're saying, Garth."

"Your old man, came to my house and threatened me with a shotgun," Garth stated flatly as he adjusted his baseball cap and hitched up his stained jeans.

"He... what?"

"You heard me."

"That's news to me," Ernie replied, feeling himself flush as he spoke.

Ernie didn't quite know what to say. He quickly recalled seeing his father's shotgun leaning against the kitchen cupboards. He also recalled not seeing the old shotgun when he racked the good one. Now he wondered, if this was true, would his father have used the good one or perhaps the old one? Why was the good shotgun in the kitchen that day; and where was the old one?

"You might want to have a talk with him," Garth said. "Because if he does it again..."

Ernie began to reply but as he did so, he brushed

against the six-foot-tall display of toilet paper. Parts of it tumbled to the floor causing Ernie to scramble to keep the entire thing from falling over. When he was sure no more would come tumbling down, he turned to face Garth to see him gone.

"What in the Bee Gees was that about?" Ernie wondered aloud. He knew his father was more than capable of doing what Garth had said but not without reason. His father was a crusty old codger, and he was getting worse as time went on. But for his ninety-three-year-old father to bother taking his shotgun with him to see Garth Blackett meant something had seriously angered his old man. Ernie reached for his cellphone in his pocket but stopped himself as he looked at the tumbled display before him.

As he rebuilt the stacked display, he recalled seeing Officers Libby and Reggie on his last visit to his father's place. The same day he noticed the shotgun in the kitchen. That's when he put it all together. His father must suspect his neighbor, Garth Blackett of having something to do with the trash on his property. That was the only thing he could come up with as he walked back to his office to fetch his keys. He had to know more and knew who best could fill him in on the goings on with his father and his not-so-charming neighbor.

Part 5

Midnight in Carlton

20

UNDER THE SOFT GLOW OF streetlights, near midnight, Clovis stopped his truck across the street from Ms. Musgrave's brightly lit festive home. He turned off the engine and smiled at his wife who had already undone her seatbelt, flipped up the center console and scooted over on the bench seat to sit next to her husband. Raylene took her husband's arm and draped it over her shoulders as she snuggled up to him as they basked in the glow of the beautiful Christmas display.

"The only thing missing is the snow," Clovis said.

"You say that every time."

"It's true."

"I'm rather enjoying it like this. We don't need to wear winter clothes or idle the truck like we used to have to do," Raylene said as she palmed away a tear.

"Ernie Woodman came to see me today," Clovis stated, changing the subject like he always did to keep from letting his emotions get to him.

"And?" Raylene asked.

"He said Garth Blackett threatened to hurt his father."

"What?" Raylene said with a startle. She pulled away and looked Clovis in the eyes. Clovis knew she was hoping to see humor in his eyes but found none.

"You're not joking, are you?" Raylene asked.

"Ernie wanted to know if his father really did go to

Garth's house armed with a shotgun."

"When did this happen?" Raylene asked, obviously wondering how she hadn't heard anything about this until now.

Clovis ignored the question and continued. "Turns out Garth Blackett is the one dumping garbage on Eli Woodman's property."

"Was there ever any doubt?" Raylene asked as she snuggled up to her husband again.

"Of course," Clovis replied as he hugged her close and kissed the top of her head. "I can't assume he's the culprit just because he's a jerk and lives next door to Eli."

"Well, he sure is the type to do something like that so *I'm* not surprised."

"True. Anyway. Turns out old Eli took the trash Garth had dumped on his property, loaded it in his old Fargo and drove it to Garth's house."

"Are you serious?"

Clovis could hear a combination of concern, amusement and disbelief in his wife's voice.

"What happened?" she asked.

"I think things might have gotten real ugly had Eli not thought to bring his old shotgun with him. Although it's good he never had to use it. Damn thing is in such sorry shape, I don't think it could be fired even if it had been loaded."

"Corn Flakes!" Raylene muttered.

Clovis smiled at his wife's favored substitute for a curse word. Sure, she slipped up occasionally but being a schoolteacher with young children had broken her off swearing a long time ago. One of the many things he adored about his wife.

"And?" Raylene asked, craning her neck, clearly wanting more details about the incident.

"Apparently Eli hadn't told Ernie about it. So, when Ernie bumped into Garth, he brought it up."

"That must have been quite a shock," Raylene said, resting her head against her husband.

"I explained to Ernie how I ordered Libby and Reggie to take Eli's shotgun. Which they did on my orders. I wanted to make that part clear."

"Can you do that?"

"Well technically, from what I gathered, old Eli never actually threatened Garth. He just happened to bring the shotgun with him. Which I figure is the only reason I didn't have to arrest Garth for assaulting a ninety-three-year-old. I figure Ernie knew this, which is why he didn't make a fuss about it."

"Remember when you used to say this town was almost too quiet?" Raylene asked.

"Nothing ever happens in Carlton," they both said in unison, smiling as they did.

"I miss those days," Clovis stated.

"So, what did Ernie say?"

"I think at that point he wasn't quite sure what to say. I offered to give him his father's shotgun, if he promised me, he wouldn't give it back to Eli until all this blew over."

"You assume this will blow over?"

"Of course. Eli and I both know; Garth was the one dumping trash on the old man's property. There's no denying it."

"Just remember this is Garth Blackett we're talking about here. Since when have you known Garth to let anything go?"

Clovis sometimes hated to admit his wife was right. Especially when he desperately wanted her to be wrong. He knew Garth was the type to hold a grudge, even if Garth himself was the one in the wrong.

"Don't tell anyone about this," Clovis said to Raylene. Something he usually didn't bother to say because he trusted her completely. But in this case, she was right, and he wanted to keep this quiet.

"Of course, I won't say anything," Raylene replied. "But you might want to make sure Libby or Reggie keep quiet too."

"They know better," Clovis said as his mind wandered

to the time he went to Garth's house, called by his battered wife to come and make sure she could leave without him trying to finally kill her. He had taken one look at her and tried to convince her to press charges, but she refused. Clovis hadn't pushed it further, fearing what would happen if she didn't stay gone. But he hated to admit, in this case, his wife was probably right about Garth. He was like a stack of dry wood. All he needed was a little fuel and the right thing to set him off and he would rage out of control. Clovis was starting to regret bringing it up and souring the moment.

"Did I tell you I spoke to Ms. Musgrave?" Clovis asked, changing the subject.

"How is she?" Raylene inquired.

"Good. Hip pain but she's taking medication for it."

"That's good."

"She was happy to see me. Made me tea and cookies."

"Well, aren't you spoiled?" Raylene said playfully.

Clovis smiled as he watched the animated Santa Clause decoration raise his arm and fake drink from a vintage 7-up bottle.

"I've never seen her so happy. Not since her husband passed away."

"It's the decorations. They make her happy. Plus, the fact that they seem to piss off the mayor."

"You heard that, did you?" Clovis asked with levity in his voice.

"Who hasn't?" Raylene replied.

Clovis couldn't see her face but knew from her tone his wife was smiling and that made him happy.

"She's such a sweetheart," Raylene added.

Clovis held his wife as he thought back to the very first time they met, at a Christmas tree lot, both looking to buy the last tree available. It was such a cheesy story, like something out of a Hallmark Christmas movie. One of those where they meet, fall in love and spend the rest of their lives together. Only nobody ever expected that to end so soon.

"Anna gets back from Paris next week," Raylene said.

"I know," Clovis replied as he palmed away a tear.

"We need to tell the kids. It's not fair to them."

"Soon," Clovis replied, hugging his wife as they continued basking in the warmth of the Christmas decorations that irritated the mayor so much.

21

Nearing the end of his first term as mayor, Jack Ledger hadn't planned on running for reelection. His wife would retire early from her job as a legal assistant, and he too had planned on retiring early as well. He would sell some properties, hire a few more people to manage some businesses he owned and retire.

The plan at the time was to bring his wife on the longest cruise he could find. She had loved the idea of getting away, just the two of them, for more than just a short vacation. They had talked about it for years. But before they could, Jack Ledger's wife passed away of sudden heart failure. Her sudden passing had left the mayor with a void in his life that would be impossible to fill. He found himself not wanting to be home alone. Their children, grown and gone, the house had felt incredibly empty without his wife of thirty-two years. And now early retirement seemed like a bad idea. So, he did what he always did, which was immerse himself in work. He had already taken to doing more of the minor renovations in his many rental properties. This helped occupy him when he had occasional vacancies. But then the idea of no longer being mayor of the town he loved so much suddenly filled him with anxiety. What would he fill his days with if he didn't have this to do? Plus, he was good at it. So, the loss of his wife had meant the town would, if they chose to, get to keep him as mayor. So, he was reelected.

But Jack still had a void in his life that he realized he could never truly fill. Although he eventually found himself wanting a human connection, even though he wouldn't admit to it. That's when Bonnie Campbell came into his life as more than just an ex-employee and owner of one of his past businesses.

In his youth, Jack didn't know anything about running a newspaper. So, he had hired someone to help him get it off the ground and run it. In the early years, with a lot of help from the staff, he clumsily oversaw the running of the small weekly newspaper. Eventually he had hired Bonnie Campbell to help with this workload when he had decided to run for mayor. He hadn't known at the time that she would eventually own the paper instead of him.

After a while, their friendship turned to passion, which he pretended was all about sex, but he was getting the intimacy he had been missing since his wife's passing. He could only assume Bonnie felt the same, as she wasn't the type to talk about feelings. Sure, sometimes he would say something stupid, and she would get mad at him. But the fling he kept secret because he feared how it would look, if the mayor had a lady friend, so soon after his wife's passing at that.

She, he assumed, kept it a secret because he was her former boss, so to keep her integrity, wanted this kept secret as well. This is the reason either of them ever slept over at the other's place. So, at almost midnight, Jack was driving through the town he felt so passionately about on his way home from a visit at Bonnie's, who had gotten over whatever it was that had made her so upset at their last encounter.

Jack slowed his car as he approached the church, noticing how the defaced rainbow crosswalk was apparent under the streetlights, even at night.

Some members of the town council debated repainting it as what they called normal again, meaning white only. They had expressed fears that vandalism would reoccur if they went with the rainbow colors again. Something many hadn't agree with as that would mean the bigots would win. Many had felt they shouldn't allow that.

This is what Jack was thinking as he slowed his car to

a crawl, driving over the gentle hill in the middle of town, in front of the Saint Francis Catholic Church as he looked at the still defaced crosswalk. And so, while preoccupied, he never saw the truck coming from behind him until it was too late.

22

Garth Blackett had never had real friends. He had friends, but not real close friends. He had spent most of his childhood as a bully and retained that reputation into his early adulthood. Eventually he matured just enough to become a functioning member of society. But the anger and resentment of not always being as great as he perceived himself to be always got just under the surface of his very thin skin. And even though many feared him, some of those that didn't teased him, poking fun at every opportunity. And if he got upset, that only fueled their fun at his expense. For some, it was sweet revenge for the years Garth spent tormenting them, their family or their friends. So, when a few people overheard him at the grocery store telling Ernie Woodman that his father, old Eli Woodman had pulled a shotgun on him, the rumor mill was set into high gear.

Some of the patrons at Burnett's Place had been eagerly waiting for Garth to come to the bar for a few beers. They had waited until he was settled on a stool by the bar, beer in hand before inquiring about his visit from Eli. A ninety-three-year-old man who had apparently put *the* Garth Blackett in his place, someone said to him. They had prodded him with a series of questions to find out why. He knew his surprised expressive reaction had revealed the shotgun incident to be true, but they hadn't known what had brought it on. Why had Garth's old neighbor felt the need to bring a shotgun?

Garth told them the only thing he could think of, which was that at ninety-three, old Eli was finally losing it. This was more than likely as Eli was known to most as an old codger. Although Eli had never been one to go looking for trouble, he had never been one to stand down when it found him, even in his old age.

Many assumed that Garth had been feeding deer and bears again, drawing wildlife into the area. Everyone knew the story of how Eli had been chased by a bear long ago. This was a plausible theory that a few preferred. But no matter how much they asked, Garth wouldn't confirm it or tell them why the old man had been to his house armed with a shotgun. And after his second beer, he had listened to enough of their questions and theories. He repeatedly insisted that Eli was going crazy and would soon have to go into a nursing home.

This is what he was thinking as he drove through town at a little over the speed limit, scanning the dark side streets for Officer Dwayne Adams who sometimes parked and watched traffic go by. With that and being deeply engrossed in the thought of Eli spreading trash all over his truck, he never saw the taillights of the sedan that was almost stopped on the gentle hill in front of the Catholic Church until it was too late. Even though Garth slammed on the brakes, it was impossible to prevent the impact.

Garth's crew cab truck was high off the ground and so his hard bumper took the impact, but the smaller, lower sedan didn't fare as well as its back end crumpled like a paper bag. The trunk lid bent in multiple places and curled upwards, towards the back window of the car.

From down a side street, red and blue police cruiser lights appeared suddenly, casting a glow on the surrounding homes and trees as it approached.

Caught in the act, Garth ignored his initial instinct of driving off. Instead, he jumped out of his truck to assess the damage. He looked under his truck for signs of coolant leaking and saw none. Looking his truck over, all he could see was the steel bumper was badly scratched, bent and skewed just enough to make sure everyone would see what had happened to him. Some idiot stopped in the middle of the road, thought Garth. None of this was his fault. How could it be? He was obeying the laws.

Garth spat and muttered a curse as he watched the police cruiser approach.

From the vehicle he had hit exited the mayor of Carlton, looking rather bewildered, thought Garth. Although he preferred to think the mayor looked stupefied. Garth's opinion of the mayor had never been very high, and this would only make it worse.

How dumb can he be, wondered Garth as he spat once more and turned to watch Officer Dwayne Adams park his car askew in the street with his cruiser lights flashing.

23

OFFICER DWAYNE ADAMS HAD been hoping for a quiet evening. He had a new book waiting for him on his desk he was anxious to get to. Working the graveyard in a sleepy little town offered him time to do what he loved best. Read. Dwayne was obsessed with stories set in small towns. He had a newly purchased copy of *Arcadia Falls* by Ken Stark waiting on his desk, but he was disheartened in the thought that he probably wouldn't get to start it this night after all.

He parked his cruiser to block the street, letting his flashing cruiser lights warn any oncoming traffic passing through the small town of the vehicles in the road. He adjusted his police issue baseball cap and stepped out of the vehicle to assess the rarity of a fender bender at this hour in the otherwise quiet of midnight on a weeknight.

Each of the drivers were now standing beside their vehicles, looking like neither of the men were injured. The vehicles he now recognized as the mayor's sedan and Garth Blackett's truck.

By the look of the vehicles, he could tell the impact hadn't been incredibly hard, although the car looked like it had taken the brunt of the damage, which wasn't surprising considering the size of the truck that hit it. The car had been pushed forward a few feet and so he could get a better look at each vehicle. Dwayne shone his flashlight under the truck, expecting to see fluid leaking from the radiator but saw none. The mayor's sedan, however, wouldn't be road worthy for a while, if ever. Dwayne assumed that the amount of damage to the rear may have also bent the frame in some way. He knelt and looked under the car for potential gas leaking and was pleased to see none. At least there was that, thought Dwayne as he heard another vehicle approaching. Turning he saw a closed-fisted Garth walking towards the mayor.

"What the hell were you thinking, stopping in the middle of the road like that?" Garth said loudly.

"How is it you didn't see me?" Jack Ledger retorted.

"So, you think this is my fault?" Garth replied incredulously.

"Guys, calm down," Dwayne stated as he watched the approaching truck swerve and come to a stop in the church parking lot.

24

"STAY HERE," CLOVIS SAID to Raylene as he shut off the truck's engine and got out to inspect the scene before him.

"Chief," Dwayne said loudly so the pair of men would hear, appearing to Clovis as if he was hoping it would help defuse the tension that had clearly been building.

"Clovis?" Mayor Jack Ledger interjected in what sounded like surprise. "What are you doing out at this hour?"

The mayor turned his attention to the Chief's truck as they heard a door shut. Raylene was now standing next to the vehicle, arms crossed.

"Is everyone alright?" they all heard her ask.

"I think so," Jack replied.

The mayor looked uncomfortable, thought Clovis as he stifled a grin knowing that Jack was suddenly wondering if he still smelled of sex, which he did.

Garth, who had been tense when Clovis first spotted

him, seemed to have relaxed a little. Most likely because now two cops were on the scene. That and he assumed Garth, who was now in the process of inspecting his truck, was happy to see he had minimal damage to what was obviously an already banged up work truck to begin with.

"How did this happen?" Clovis asked, glancing back and forth between Jack and Garth, assessing their body language as well as facial expressions.

"I was just about to ask the same thing," Dwayne added.

"This asshole was practically stopped in the middle of the road," Garth said just before he lay on the asphalt to look under his truck, continuing his inspection.

"I wasn't stopped," Jack Ledger replied. "I admit, I had slowed down quite a bit."

"And you didn't see him?" Clovis asked as he pulled his phone from his hip holster and snapped a picture of Garth's truck. He looked disappointingly at the dark picture.

"Turn the flash back on," he heard his wife say.

This reminded him that, with a little guidance from his loving wife, he had previously turned it off. He had done that when he took a picture of Ms. Musgrave's brightly illuminated festive house. He turned the flash on and proceeded to hastily take a series of pictures of both vehicles.

"Did anyone call Clark's Towing?" Clovis inquired calmly, as if this happened all the time.

"I don't need a tow," Garth said as he scrambled out from under his truck.

"I can see that," Clovis replied. "But Clark will take a quick look for me to be sure."

"I might be able to drive it home," Jack said, obviously referring to his own vehicle.

"Maybe," Clovis replied as he shot a glance at Dwayne, who took the hint and went to his cruiser to call for a tow truck. "But best not to."

Clovis turned to Raylene. "Go home. I'll get a ride back with Dwayne when we're done here."

"I don't mind waiting," Raylene replied.

"I know, hun. But this could take a while. I'll let you know when I'm on my way so you can make Dwayne and I some tea… please?"

"Sure," Raylene replied with what sounded like reluctance.

"God, I love that woman," Clovis muttered as he watched her get into the driver's side of his truck and adjust the seat so she could reach the pedals.

25

As Raylene adjusted the seat to her liking, which was as close as it could get, she watched her husband turn his attention to the mayor of the little town they all loved so much. She knew after spending time basking in the glow of the Christmas lights, this had left Clovis feeling sentimental, which always led to him feeling as if he needed to protect her. He didn't mean to come off as condescending, this she knew. She understood that when he let himself feel, he became super protective of those he loved, especially his wife and kids. Plus, he was right that there was nothing she could do here except distract her husband and he clearly wanted to stay with Dwayne. He was probably worried that Garth might work himself into a frenzy, if he wasn't there to keep him calm. Dwayne was a good cop, great in fact. But he was still young, in Clovis's eyes. He often said so.

But as she started the truck, she couldn't help but wonder how long it would take her husband to bring up the topic of the vandalized sign in Pleasant Ridge.

Clovis had been after his old schoolmate, the mayor and city council to repaint or replace the *Welcome to Carlton* sign which had been spray-painted. He had been after them about this for a long time. He had even raised the money to have it done. But for reasons he couldn't understand, they had been putting it off. Now she suddenly found herself wanting this done as well. Not for the same reasons as her husband. She wanted it done so *he* could let this go.

She smiled as the solution to this came to her just now. She knew how to get this done sooner rather than later. Clovis might not like it if he knew this would be her doing. Not at first anyway but what the hell, she thought while driving home. After all, it was midnight in Carlton, the cops were busy for a while and in the end, he would finally get this resolved. This is what mattered, she thought while palming away a fresh tear while heading home with a sudden mission in mind.

Part 6

A Good Talking To

26

"I CAN'T BELIEVE THE CHIEF didn't tell you about the mayor's fender bender," Dwayne said as he put on his hat and sat at his desk in the police bullpen. He spun his chair to face Libby who had just sat down with her first Santorene coffee of the day.

"He doesn't tell me much anymore," Libby replied as she gripped her precious coffee in both hands, holding it near her face while inhaling the aroma of the coffee.

"It was two days ago," Dwayne replied.

"Ever since…" Libby began saying before stopping herself. She still couldn't say it aloud. She sipped at her coffee to keep from getting emotional. "He probably hasn't done anything about it anyway."

"I don't think there's much to be done," Dwayne replied. "The mayor's car got the worst of it. Garth's truck didn't look to be damaged at all. Maybe a few scratches on the bumper."

"That's good, considering it was Garth Blackett. I mean he would have freaked out if his truck had gotten serious damage. Especially since it was the mayor who was stopped in the middle of the road."

"He wasn't actually stopped," Dwayne corrected.

Libby ignored the comment and continued.

"Garth already hates the mayor as it is so this couldn't have helped any," Libby said as she sipped coffee.

"I expected him to be much more upset than he was. But I think he was a little proud that his truck didn't really get damaged while the mayor's sedan looked like a write off."

"I could see that," Libby replied. "He's that type. Like his truck is somehow an extension of his manhood. Like he somehow has something to do with its existence. Like he built the damned thing instead of buying it like everyone else."

Dwayne smiled, showing amusement at one of Libby's pet peeves. But the smile only lasted for a moment before he became serious again.

"You think we should talk to the chief?" he asked.

"Yes, I think we need to," Libby replied as she choked up, coughed to clear her throat and continued. "But I can't."

"I know. Me either," Dwayne replied glumly. "But we really should."

Libby sipped coffee while staring at Dwayne who retrieved his book from his desk. He thumbed through it quietly for a moment before breaking the awkward silence.

"We should. He's neglecting a lot of things."

"I know. He really should have made the Eli Garth thing official instead of sweeping it under the rug," Libby said setting her coffee down and booting up her computer.

"I don't think he's done any paperwork or anything at all about the crosswalk," Dwayne replied.

"He was supposed to give me the pictures he took," Libby added. "I haven't seen them yet."

"Eli's shotgun is still in his office," Dwayne said.

"Reggie reminded me of that yesterday. He's nervous he'll get in trouble for taking it."

"He might," Dwayne said.

"Clovis told us to take it. Ordered us to," Libby replied. "I had to remind Reggie of that. I think Clovis did that so we wouldn't get in trouble."

"Still," Dwayne said as he got to his feet, fondled his

book awkwardly as he spoke. "The chief needs a good talking to."

"Soon," Libby replied as she typed in her password and opened her email. "But not today, okay?"

27

Years ago, Garth Blackett had moved away for a spell. This had been his way of trying to distance himself from his past—literally. And while he tried, this ended up not working because he wasn't as mature as he thought he was. It didn't take long before he got into trouble and was forced to admit to himself that he was better off where he had grown up. Even if over half the town hated him and the rest didn't care if he existed at all. At least there, most people avoided him, and this helped keep trouble at bay.

But he had to work for a living and Garth Blackett was a heavy equipment operator. This meant he had to go where the work was. Job site locations varied and so being gone for weeks, sometimes months was his normal and helped keep him out of trouble. His favorite part about this was working with strangers. People who wouldn't constantly remind him of how much of an ass he was to them in their youth. Another helpful part of being a heavy machine operator meant being alone a lot, in the cab of a dozer, backhoe or whatever he was operating at the time. So, when a local job opportunity came up to help build cranberry bogs, he assumed, being alone in a cab of heavy equipment might make it possible for him to work near home for a while. He liked the idea since being able to live in his own house meant less expenses so he might make a little more money.

That and he liked the idea of being a part of the new cranberry operations starting up in the outskirts of his hometown. This would give him some personal satisfaction from taking part in something most viewed as positive for the community. It might make people more tolerant of him, he had thought. More accepting and perhaps help him move on from his past. And while Garth tried hard to make the best of working near home, his reputation somehow always found a way to haunt him.

The new rumors of his troubles with his elderly neighbor reached his workplace through lunch at the Santorene diner. The coworkers who had experienced torment from Garth back in their school years saw an opportunity. A few members of the crew in charge of building the irrigation system to flood the bogs had heard the rumors. And Joshua, being a cousin to Ernie Woodman, was assigned the task of looking into it. Joshua thought if the rumors were true that Ernie needed a good talking to about his aging father.

28

ERNIE WOODMAN HAD HEARD about the trash incident by accidental admission from Garth himself and so confronted his aging father about it soon after. His father confessed to returning Garth Blackett's trash which he had found on his property. Trash which he now knew clearly belonged to his neighbor. And when Ernie asked his father about bringing a shotgun, his father simply smiled and changed the subject. Ernie could only assume that was why Chief Clovis and his officers had confiscated the old shotgun. But one thing Ernie knew was his father, even though he was now ninety-three, still had all his wits about him.

Physically, his father had declined a lot in the last decade. Albeit he still drove around his property on his old Case L Tractor, but he had stopped cutting and hauling firewood or planting a garden. He had the mental capacity but now lacked the physical ability. So, the idea of his father taking an old shotgun that he knew couldn't be of any use to Garth's house was ridiculous. Perhaps twenty years ago, old Eli would have done this. To scare his neighbor without accidentally shooting him in the process. But at ninety-three, he would have brought his good shotgun, and it would have been loaded. In his state, he would have known he wouldn't be able to fight a man like Garth. He would have brought the right tool for the job. One of his father's favorite old sayings. And this would have explained why the new shotgun was in the kitchen and not on the rack that day. Plus, it explained why officers Libby and Reggie saw the old shotgun on the rack and assumed this was what he had used. Therefore, Clovis still had the old shotgun but the new one was at his father's house still on the gun rack in the living room. This made sense now, as much as it could. His father was known as a crazy coot to many, but Ernie knew better. His father needed a good talking to, but every time Ernie tried, his father would change the subject. Eli was old but still very sly.

So, when Ernie's cousin Joshua caught him off-guard, Ernie got flustered and attempted to defend his father's actions.

"Is it true?" Joshua blurted when he found Ernie in the produce section.

Ernie paused in his task of reorganizing the stacked 10-pound bags of Russet potatoes to see who was speaking to him.

"Is it true?" Joshua repeated. "Did Uncle Eli pull a shotgun on Garth Blackett?"

Finding himself flustered at the idea that his cousin knew about this, Ernie blurted out a response he quickly wished he could take back.

"Garth should know better than to dump trash on my dad's land."

"He did what?"

Ernie realized then that Joshua only knew about the what and not the why.

"He dumped trash on Uncle Eli's property? Oh, this is rich!" Joshua exclaimed with glee. "The guys at the bog are going to love this one."

Ernie watched dumbfounded as a smiling Joshua left as abruptly as he had appeared.

Ernie knew he shouldn't have said anything. If anything, he had just thrown fuel on the fire that was the feud between his father and his neighbor.

"Crap!" Ernie spat loudly as he picked up a bag of potatoes without knowing it had a tear in it, only to see the spuds tumble out, roll off the other bags and spill to the floor. Ernie sighed, bent to pick up the potatoes as he realized that he needed to give his father a good talking to and soon to avoid this escalating.

29

IT DIDN'T TAKE LONG for Joshua to fill his coworkers in on what had happened between Garth and his crotchety old uncle. He regaled them with tales of his once rugged uncle who was still kicking enough to apparently put Garth Blackett in his place. He exaggerated stories of his uncle's past fearlessness around bears and coyote. Most of these stories were based on small truths but blown out proportion to make his old uncle seem heroic, as he now viewed him. This old man, in his nineties—Joshua couldn't recall exactly how old his uncle was—had faced a man most of them still felt anxiety just being around. Sure, he wasn't the bully he once was, but Garth still walked and talked with an attitude. They had to convince themselves it was mostly bluster as there were consequences that adults had to face that kids in school could get away with. But revenge was something they couldn't pass up, even if it was enacted anonymously.

Through a joint effort, it didn't take more than a day for the crew to gather enough trash bags to fill the box of Garth's crew cab truck. And at the end of the workday, they gathered near it so they could see their old bully's reaction.

30

"WHICH ONE OF YOU pricks did this?" Garth barked

when he saw the box of his truck was filled with transparent trash bags. He turned to see most of the crew milling about more than usual, instead of rushing off as normal on a Friday night at quitting time.

"Joshua," Garth barked as he spotted his old schoolmate in the throng. "Was this you?"

Garth's anger rose as he marched up to his truck, opened the driver's side door and threw in his lunch box. He turned to face his coworkers with every intention of tearing into them to find out who had done this when he spotted the site foreman among the gaggle. He knew the foreman wouldn't tolerate another angry outburst. He was on thin ice with him about tardiness and his attitude towards coworkers. The foreman had given him a good talking to on more than a few occasions about not treating them as inferior. If he let loose now, Garth knew he would get fired. Instead, he jumped into his truck and smashed down the accelerator as he drove off the job site. As his truck swerved on the road, he could see the trash bags sliding around in the box in his rearview mirror. This only had the effect of making his blood boil.

Part 7

It's a Sign

31

JUST PAST FIVE ON A Friday afternoon, Chief Clovis removed his cap, scratched his head through his predominantly graying hair and smiled at the sight before him. He couldn't help but wonder why he hadn't thought of this himself.

A 'bloop' sound made him reach for his cell phone holster instinctively. He was looking at his phone before he even realized he had pulled it out. He read the text from his wife.

"Can I call you?"

He called her.

"Is everything okay?" Clovis inquired without hesitation.

"Is this a bad time?" Raylene asked in reply.

"Not at all."

"I just spoke to Anna. She said she loved Paris but misses home. She's flying back the day after tomorrow."

"Good," Clovis replied. "We should drive up to Stonevalley to pick her up at the airport."

"Actually, Jaffer is picking her up," Raylene replied, referring to their daughter's boyfriend. "I convinced her to come home for a visit as soon as she lands."

"She won't come home without him?" Clovis asked, leaning back and perching himself on the edge of the hood of his cruiser to take the weight off his sore leg.

"I told her to bring him. I think it's time we met him anyway. They've been dating almost a year now."

"I met him once. Before they started dating," Clovis replied. "Seven long years ago, in Stonevalley."

"That's right," Raylene replied. "The time you picked up Anna on campus, just before the Burnett thing," Raylene said. It was one of the few times he had picked up their independent daughter.

"Speaking of which, you'll never guess what I just found."

"Don't make me guess. I hate that," Raylene replied.

Clovis smiled as he heard amusement in his wife's voice.

"I'm out in Pleasant Ridge," Clovis replied.

Clovis heard a rustling sound from the other end of the call and then dead air for a moment making him wonder if he had lost the call. He looked at the screen and saw that the call looked to be active still.

"Hello? Honey? You still there?"

"I'm here," Raylene replied.

Clovis thought she suddenly sounded as if something was off. Although he wasn't sure. There were a lot of days she sounded like this now. They had a lot to deal with and so her mood swings were to be expected. Besides, he was about to give her what he considered to be good news. Great news, in fact.

"The mayor and city council finally won't have a choice but fix the sign out in Pleasant Ridge," Clovis added cheerily.

Clovis heard Raylene shuffling about as she spoke.

"What makes you say that?" she asked.

He heard what he figured was the fridge open and close. Heard what he thought was the sound of his wife drinking something.

"Someone torched the town limit sign. There's not much of it left," Clovis replied as he examined the remains of the sign.

Someone had clearly covered it in accelerant and set it

ablaze. Parts of it were completely burnt away, while most of what remained was charred. Only the lower portion of one of the posts supporting it was partially unscathed. Patches of grass around it had also burned.

"It's amazing the fire didn't spread to the grass. Or worse, out of control," Clovis added.

"True. But maybe now you'll finally be able to let that go," Raylene replied meekly.

"Thanks to whoever burned it. Yes. I believe I will," Clovis replied gleefully.

"I'm glad," he heard his wife reply with emotion in her voice.

"It's a sign," Clovis said, smiling at his own lame joke. But it worked as he heard his wife guffaw on the other end of the call.

"I'll be home shortly," he added before ending the call.

Using his phone, he snapped a few pictures of the remains of the town limit sign. Smiling as he examined the images, the thought of Jack Ledger seeing the sign like this made him almost giddy. If only the mayor was here now. Clovis wished he could see the look on his face when he saw this. That's when he decided it couldn't wait, smiling as he texted the mayor a simple message.

"It's a sign," the text read, which he followed by sending the picture of the charred remains of the town limit sign.

The reply text came swiftly.

"WTF?" Jack replied.

Clovis smiled as he holstered his phone, got in his cruiser and headed for home.

32

Just past six on a Friday afternoon, Garth Blackett sat at his kitchen table, angrily chewing a mouthful of pizza from Skipper Jacks. He swallowed and bit into the pizza slice, also accidentally biting the inside of his cheek as well, for the second time since he sat down to supper. He set the pizza down, picked up the full soda can at his side. Seething with rage, he threw it as hard as he could, making it explode against the kitchen wall coating the area with soda. It impacted inches away from the widow over the sink. The empty can clattered off the counter and settled on the floor.

Ignoring the dent in the drywall and the foaming and dripping soda he stuck a finger in his mouth poking at the spot he had just bitten for the second time. Removing his finger, he examined it and saw blood. His blood. Accidentally biting the inside of his cheek was something he had done plenty of times. He blamed his missing back teeth for this whenever it happened. But when he did it a second time, it always made him angry.

Angry at whom? Himself, mostly was the answer. And now his pizza would taste like blood.

He boiled with rage, thinking about this and how the guys had been laughing when he drove off the job site with his truck box filled with garbage bags. Garbage bags that were still there. He had wanted to swing by the town dumpster after picking up pizza, but he had forgotten. Now the trash sat there, taunting him, a reminder of the bullshit he had put up with lately. *It was a sign or something*, he thought, picking up the pizza slice and gingerly taking a bite, chewing slowly while breathing deeply through his nose, trying to calm himself.

It was a sign that he shouldn't let the old coot get the better of him or he would never live it down. This is what he was thinking when he wiped his mouth with a Skipper Jack's napkin and saw blood on it.

33

JUST PAST SEVEN ON a Friday evening, Bonnie Campbell stood before the recently charred town limit sign in Pleasant Ridge. She snapped pictures of the remains of the sign using a small but powerful digital camera, examining each picture after taking it, looking for the perfect combination of angle and light. She paused as she saw a vehicle approaching. She didn't recognize the white SUV as it crossed the road and parked on the other side of the sign. She tensed at first until she saw Mayor Jack Ledger emerging from the unfamiliar vehicle.

"It's a rental," Jack muttered as he walked over and stood next to Bonnie, facing the remains of the town limit sign.

Bonnie grimaced as she spoke. "You know anything about this?"

"Only what Clovis told me a few hours ago. That someone had clearly covered it in accelerant and set it on fire."

"I swear the whole town has gone crazy. I remember when Carlton was so damned quiet," Bonnie replied.

"Look on the bright side," Jack replied. "This will certainly help the newspaper."

Bonnie glanced at Jack with raised eyebrows, her disbelief apparent.

"I can't not write about this," Bonnie said as she tucked the camera into her large purse that dangle off her shoulder and pulled out a notepad and pen. "This is the second act of vandalism in less than a week."

"Second?" Jack asked.

"The crosswalk?" Bonnie said incredulously. "How could you forget about that?"

"Oh. Right."

"You're amazing," Bonnie muttered as she jotted down details in her notebook.

Jack glanced over her shoulder to see his name noted at the top of the page. Next to it, Bonnie had noted Chief Clovis McPhee.

"So how long do you think it will take the council to get the sign replaced?" Bonnie asked in what sounded like an official tone of voice.

"I have no idea," Jack replied. "I don't even think they know about this yet. But I wouldn't be surprised if Clovis didn't call them after I spoke to him. You know what he told me? He said it was a sign."

Bonnie smirked at the pun that probably had gone over the mayor's head. Clovis was always making quirky jokes. This annoyed Bonnie but she also loved this about Clovis. It was as if he didn't take himself too seriously. Bonnie jotted this down as it might make a great headline.

"*Chief Clovis McPhee calls vandalism a sign,*" she noted. She wondered if that would work, suddenly glad she had stopped at the gas station on her way out here and had run into Dwayne.

"He's right about that part," Bonnie said. "It is a sign."

"At least it was," Jack replied, grinning slightly.

Bonnie, seeing the smile, realized that Jack had just gotten the joke.

Part 8

All's Well That Ends Well?

34

RAYLENE HADN'T LIKED THAT CLOVIS wanted to take care of something this Saturday morning. She had wanted to spend a quiet morning with her husband, just the two of them. Maybe do something like drive out to the lake for a picnic. This is what she had told him to which he replied that they would. He just had one person he wanted to visit, and he wanted to do it in uniform. He had put it off too long already.

So early on this partly cloudy Saturday morning, Chief Clovis McPhee pulled his police cruiser into Garth Blackett's gravel driveway and parked behind the large truck with the barely damaged bumper. As he got out of his cruiser, he glanced at the house and saw movement behind the window in the front door.

Garth was awake like he had assumed. Unless he had gotten completely drunk the night before, which was a possibility. Otherwise, these construction guys were hardwired as early risers.

Limping past the truck, Clovis paused and examined its empty box. He recalled how full of trash it had been when he had last been here. Clovis knew that Garth had called them thinking they would arrest Eli Woodman. That's what he had told Libby they should do when he called about the trash and the shotgun. Clovis knew that Garth had tried to handle the situation in a way that wouldn't result in his getting into trouble. Something that backfired since the trash was clearly his in the first place. Also, Garth hadn't known that Eli had complained to the cops about trash being dumped on his property. It was obvious to Clovis that Garth had assumed he would get away with it. How was Garth to know that his ninety-three-year-old neighbor was still spry enough to wander the back parts of his property? Or that he was sharp enough to figure out where the trash had come from.

Clovis placed his hand on his gun as he heard the screen door clack shut. A scruffy-looking Garth was now standing on his stoop, holding a coffee mug in one hand.

"What's the problem now?" Garth asked before sipping what Clovis hoped was coffee. Garth was wearing dirty looking jeans and a plaid shirt. Clovis wondered if Garth owned anything else.

Clovis sighed as he walked closer, stopping in front of the truck where he could see Garth as well as keep an eye on the house. He watched Garth's body language as he spoke.

"I been meaning to come see you," Clovis stated. "Ernie Woodman came to see me the other day."

He saw Garth swallow and shift his footing, his eyes cast down briefly as he replied. "So?"

"He said you told him about Eli coming to see you. That you asked him if his father had a death wish."

Clovis was never a big believer in body language. He understood even more now that some things can make someone exhibit behavior that had nothing to do with anything being said. He thought this as he shifted his own stance to alleviate the weight on his sore leg. And even though he was a skeptic about this, he couldn't help but feel Garth looked nervous just now, fidgeting slightly.

"Maybe he is tired of living," Garth replied, obviously trying to sound nonchalant. The chief knew he wasn't hiding his disappointment well. It had to be written all over his face as he heard Garth's disparaging reply.

"I mean come on," Garth added. "The old fucker came

to my house with a shotgun, waving it around."

"I was hoping this would blow over," Clovis said impatiently. "That you would be mature about this and stop with the stupid shit. I tried, Garth. I tried to keep this quiet. But you had to tell Ernie."

Garth stood motionless, as if he was contemplating what he was hearing but Clovis knew better. He knew that someone with Garth's temperament was beginning to simmer. He was getting angry and Clovis could see it on his face as he spoke, raising his voice slightly to get his point across.

"Are you listening, Garth? I need you to let this go. You got caught and that's that. All's well that ends well, Garth!" Clovis quoted Shakespeare. "I need this to be done. I need to be able to tell Ernie that he doesn't have to worry about his father."

Clovis watched Garth tense up and then relax, as if he knew arguing or protesting wasn't a good idea.

"Can you do that?" Clovis asked, speaking normally now.

"If the old man doesn't come here with a shotgun again, sure."

"Don't give him reason to," Clovis said sternly. "All's well that ends well," he repeated before taking his leave.

35

AT NINE AM ON Saturday morning, standing next to Bonnie Campbell's bed, Mayor Jack Ledger inserted a leg into a pant leg, staggered and almost fell over. He leaned against the bedroom wall and inserted the second leg, pulling up the pants as he spoke.

"What's this I hear about you making the paper online only?" Jack asked.

Bonnie fluffed her pillow and pulled a blanket over herself as she replied to the question with one of her own.

"You remember when you hired me to help run the paper?"

"When I was getting ready to run for mayor for the first time."

"There were four of us, running the paper, not including you."

"Of course, I remember that. You were better at selling ads than the rest of the team combined," Jack said as he tucked in his dress shirt and buckled his belt.

Bonnie smiled briefly before continuing. "The paper wasn't making any money even back then. And it's been going downhill ever since."

Jack lay on the bed next to Bonnie as he continued his protest of what he believed was a terrible idea.

"Don't you think that will kill the paper?"

"It's already dying, Jack. I mean, I can't afford employees anymore and have to do it all myself."

"What about that kid you hired last year?" Jack asked.

"He was a summer student. I told everyone I hired him to help me run the paper but what I really hired him for was to teach me things."

Jack scratched himself through his pants and grunted his surprise.

"I needed to learn how to use Facebook so I could run a page myself. Also, I had him help me get a new website that I could insert articles in. Computers are not my friend, you know."

Again, Jack grunted in reply.

"I needed help to get the paper set up so I could keep it going on my own," Bonnie stated. "You hired me because I was a good reporter and good at sales too."

"You still are," Jack replied.

"But small newspapers are struggling," Bonnie replied while starring at the ceiling. "I can't afford employees anymore. I barely make enough to pay my own salary. I've had to cut out all the fluff from the paper too."

"I still think you should have kept the crossword puzzle," muttered Jack.

"Those cost money. Same with those cartoon puzzles I used to publish. The guy didn't charge much but it was still an expense that I could cut. And in cutting that, it also meant more space for ads."

"You could retire," Jack stated.

"And do what, Jack?"

"I don't know. Maybe work on that book you said you wanted to write."

"Who am I kidding, Jack. I can't write a book."

"You're a great writer," Jack replied without hesitation.

"Articles, sure. Ads, of course. But a book?"

"Why not?" Jack asked.

"Maybe something non-fiction," Bonnie said punctuating this with a sigh. "Maybe I could write about Carlton and its history. How it used to be big in Brussels sprouts farming."

Jack smirked, scratched himself again as he spoke.

"I can't retire, Jack. I'll go crazy."

"Then don't," Jack replied.

"The paper is starting to lose money so unless I want to work for free, I have to do something."

"I still think not printing it is a bad idea."

"You don't even buy ads for your vacant apartments anymore," Bonnie added.

Jack swallowed hard. She was right. He hadn't had to in years. Vacant apartments in a small town were rented most often through word of mouth. Especially since everyone had a phone on them all the time. And with the internet, it was faster for word to spread than to wait for the next print edition of the Carlton Gazette. Bonnie had a point, thought Jack.

"Not everyone is on Facebook, you know," Jack said. "I'm not."

"It's not like I want to stop printing the paper."

"Then don't."

"I can't afford not to," Bonnie replied. "People just don't support the paper like they used to. News gets spread a lot faster online. That's why I had to make a page for the paper."

"I suppose," Jack replied. "Let me think about this. I'll

try and figure something out."

"Well, if you have any ideas, I'd love to hear them."

"I'll see what I can come up with."

Bonnie got up, slipped on a housecoat and headed for the bathroom.

Jack got up and headed for the kitchen.

"Coffee?" he called as he bent to the task of making it.

"Sure," Bonnie shouted from the bathroom.

"Did you write that article about the sign yet?"

"Not yet," Bonnie replied.

"Front page?"

"Probably," Bonnie replied.

"I still can't believe you want to stop printing the paper."

"Everything doesn't always end well," Bonnie stated as she walked into the kitchen. She put a hand up to fluff her freshly brushed white hair.

"Black?" Jack asked, knowing that Bonnie had switched the way she took her coffee. They'd already had the talk of how cream reminded her too much of Baileys Irish Cream.

"Yes, please," Bonnie replied.

"I like your hair," Jack stated as he handed her a cup of black coffee.

"You're a little late with that, if you're trying to flatter me." Bonnie smiled as she sipped coffee.

Jack leaned against the kitchen counter and sipped from a mug that read, **World's Best Writener**. A gag gift Bonnie had gotten from a close friend.

36

CLOVIS PULLED THE CRUISER into his driveway and parked next to his truck. On the left, he saw his lawn tractor in the middle of the expansive lawn to the side of their home. Raylene had been out cutting the lawn again. She used to leave this chore for him but had taken on the task recently so he wouldn't have to. She wanted him to have more time to rest. She wanted more time with him. And he didn't have the heart to tell her he enjoyed cutting grass. The tranquil monotonous drone of the lawn tractor humming through his ear protection combined with what he thought of as a mindless task, calmed him. But since she was a teacher and would be off for much of this summer, he refrained from arguing with her about it. Plus, she always did a good job. She even cleaned and maintained the tractor after using it. Usually, she put it away as well. Although today, the lawn tractor was sitting in the middle of the field.

He shifted his gaze to the open two car garage at the end of the driveway and saw it was empty. Her car should be there, he thought. She should be home, waiting for his return. She had insisted on going on a picnic, just the two of them. Although she hadn't said anything about cutting the grass, he thought. He could only assume she had been a bit restless and upset over his insistence on this task that couldn't wait. A part of him wanted to admit that perhaps she was right. It could have waited until Monday. But then Garth would have been on the job, among coworkers and a visit from the chief of police might have given them something to torment the temperamental Garth with. This is the part he left out when he told his wife he felt it couldn't wait. The part about how if he spoke to Garth in a public setting, it would be like throwing fuel on a fire you were trying to extinguish.

His phone blooped, signaling a text had come in. He scooped up the phone from the passenger seat and quickly checked it.

"What are you doing?" it read.

"Just got home," he replied. "Where are you?"

"Get changed," she replied.

"Yes, dear," he texted in reply.

"I'll be home soon," she texted him. "I went to get gas for the lawnmower."

He smiled when he found the picnic basket his wife had prepared, waiting on the kitchen table. While upstairs, changing into jeans and a casual plaid shirt, he glanced out the window and saw his wife's car pull into the driveway and disappear into the garage. He heard the car door shut and watched her emerge and head straight for the lawn tractor. It was out of gas like he had assumed. That explained why she had left it in the field. He watched as she poured gas into the tractor. He tucked his shirt and limped down the stairs and into the kitchen. He turned on the coffee maker and began prepping it as he heard the lawn tractor roar to life.

He paused as he reached for cups. He recalled filling the small gas can a few days ago, after he and his wife had discussed the upcoming weekend. He had planned on cutting the lawn, first thing Saturday morning. That was before plans changed. But the tractor still had a little fuel in it and the full can should have been more than enough, yet she had run out of fuel.

He placed the cups on the counter, flicked on the coffee maker and listened to it begin to percolate.

She had gone to get fuel for the tractor, meaning the can was empty.

The can he had filled a few days ago.

Filled with an accelerant.

His heart sunk at the idea of his wife, a beloved schoolteacher, setting the town limit sign in Pleasant Ridge on fire. That would explain why the fuel can was empty. She had a clear window of opportunity while he was helping Dwayne with the accident in front of the church, thought Clovis. She could have gone home, grabbed the can of fuel, driven out to the sign and set it ablaze and made it back home before anyone noticed.

Clovis smirked at the thought.

She could have set it ablaze and gotten away with it, and in doing so made it so that the mayor and city council didn't have a choice but replace the vandalized city limit sign. It wasn't how he envisioned this ending, but it would certainly do the trick, he thought.

Clovis smiled at his wife as she entered the house.

"You know I can cut the lawn later," he stated.

"I know but I wanted us to have time together today, before Anna gets home."

"Go get changed," Clovis said as he kissed his wife and playfully patted her behind. "I'm making us some coffee."

As he heard her heading for the bedroom, he smiled again at the thought of the woman he loved burning the town limit sign. The ultimate crime of passion, he thought as she clearly would have done it for him. He would still be smiling when she returned to the kitchen, ready for their picnic. He brushed off her questions about his cheerfulness.

"I'm happy to be home, with you," he told her before kissing Raylene on the forehead.

Part 9

Linked?

37

HAVING FINISHED HER SECOND COFFEE of the morning, Libby turned her cruiser around and headed back to the station. The chief had called everyone in, even Dwayne who would have just been getting home after his graveyard shift. She hadn't expected the chief to be in for another hour, as had become his usual ever since things changed.

Libby didn't waste any time getting to the station. She marched in only to stop in the doorway of Chief Clovis McPhee's office. There she saw Dwayne sitting in a chair across from the chief while Reggie stood in the corner, perched against a filing cabinet. Both men already there, waiting on her she assumed. A clearly irritated Chief Clovis, sitting behind the desk.

"You wanted to see us?" Libby asked, trying to decide what had gotten the Chief so irritated as she stepped into the office.

Clovis opened a desk drawer, pulled out a copy of the latest Carlton Gazette and plopped it face up on the desk.

"Which one of you said this?" he asked firmly.

Libby glanced at that morning's paper. She hadn't seen it until now. Her copy was still in its bundle with the weekly flyers, sitting on the floor of her house; next to the front door where she often tossed it when she was heading off to work.

The headline made it obvious as to why the chief was upset.

`Carlton Police believe vandalism and arson linked.`

Dwayne shifted in his chair as he spoke. "I was—"

"NO!" Clovis barked, cutting him off.

Libby didn't hide her being startled as she glanced back and forth between Dwayne and Clovis.

"You don't get to make statements like this without going through me first," Clovis stated. "I'm still the chief."

"I didn't say it officially," Dwayne blurted.

Libby thought he sounded defensive, as if trying to diminish the situation.

"I was at the gas station, gassing up the cruiser. Bonnie was there too, getting gas. We were chatting," Dwayne explained.

"Anything you say, while in uniform, is official, Dwayne." Clovis plopped his hand heavily onto the thin newspaper and pivoted it to face Dwayne. "Especially if it's to Bonnie frickin Campbell."

"All I said was that I wouldn't be surprised if they were linked," Dwayne muttered with eyes downcast.

"Well, they're not," Clovis blurted. "Trust me."

"We don't really know that," Libby interjected.

"Trust me. I know," Clovis said as he glanced at Libby. "Now I gotta try and talk Bonnie into printing a retraction in the next edition which only comes out in a frickin' week."

Clovis stood abruptly, pushing his chair into the wall behind him and limped out of his office.

Reggie locked eyes with Libby as he shrugged.

Dwayne sank in the chair as he muttered. "My wife's gonna love this one."

"I was afraid we were about to have the talk," Libby said quietly as she glanced behind her to see Clovis walking out the door of the station.

"How does he know for sure the arson and the vandalism aren't linked?" Dwayne asked.

"I don't know," Libby replied. "But he seemed pretty sure of himself."

38

BONNIE SAT AT HER desk in the Carlton Gazette office, craving a drink. She closed her eyes and breathed deeply. Libby had just called to warn her about hurricane Clovis. According to Libby, Clovis had stormed off.

Would he show up in person or call, wondered Bonnie?

Libby said that Clovis had chewed out Dwayne about telling her that he thought the town limit sign arson was more than likely linked to the rainbow crosswalk vandalism. A part of her felt a little bad for Dwayne, after the fact. He was, after all, simply making small talk. But he had been on duty when she had seen him at the gas station. And it wasn't like he didn't know who she was. She had asked questions, and he had been more than happy to answer them. As a matter of fact, he more or less volunteered information. Although he did say he wouldn't be surprised that the two incidents were linked, thought Bonnie.

Her eyes still closed, Bonnie exhaled slowly through pursed lips and then inhaled deeply via nasal passage.

The old-fashioned ring tone on her cellphone startled her, breaking her attempt at alleviating the craving. Quitting drinking was proving more difficult than she cared to admit, even to herself. A quick glance at the phone confirmed the call was from the mayor. She ignored the call, letting it go to voicemail, closed her eyes and breathed deeply yet again.

Bonnie had never considered herself a true alcoholic. She drank a lot, sure. But during her occasional dry spells, she didn't get severe withdrawal symptoms like real alcoholics do. But the cravings were strong. She didn't need to drink. This is what she told herself just now, even if deep down she knew it wasn't true.

Eyes closed again, Bonnie exhaled slowly through her pursed lips and then inhaled deeply through her sinuses again. Again, the old-fashioned ring tone on her cellphone startled her. She scooped up the phone, answered the call and barked into the phone.

"Now's not a good time, Jack. If you're horny, go jerk off or something!"

Bonnie hung up the phone before Jack could say anything.

She set the phone down, closed her eyes, laid her hands flat on her desk and breathed deeply. Again, the old-fashioned ring tone on her cellphone chimed although this time it didn't startled her.

She glared at the phone and saw the caller ID wasn't Mayor Jack Ledger. Instead, it was Chief Clovis McPhee.

Bonnie swallowed hard and sent the call to voicemail.

With a few swift motions, she checked her call history and saw that the last caller hadn't been Mayor Jack Ledger after all. It had been Chief Clovis McPhee. She had told the chief of police to go jerk off.

The room began to spin as a bout of anxiety welled up inside her. She steadied herself and decided.

"I need a drink!" Bonnie said aloud, grabbed her keys, stuffed her phone into her purse and headed for her car.

39

CLOVIS SAT IN HIS cruiser, which he had parked in front of what was left of the recently burnt town limit sign in in Pleasant Ridge.

He had lied to his wife just now and it was eating away at him.

He had told her he was looking into something, and he wouldn't be home for his morning coffee break for a little while. He hadn't wanted to tell her where he really was. At the scene of the crime. Her crime. Although he hadn't made it an official crime scene just yet as the paperwork was still on his desk.

Neglecting trivial things had become a habit. Maybe this wasn't trivial to people like Bonnie Campbell, the mayor or even his police force, but it was to him.

Nobody had gotten hurt.

The only thing that was destroyed was set to be repainted, perhaps even replaced anyway. And considering all that was going on in his life at the moment, a burnt sign on the edge of town that needed replacing, felt rather trivial.

He felt, the same way about the black paint dumped on the rainbow crosswalk.

Nobody had gotten hurt. Emotions may have been stirred in some, sure. His old schoolmate, the mayor was again, proud to tell you he had predicted something like this would happen. Bonnie Campbell wrote an article that ordinarily he would have thought of as divisive. She had blasted the perpetrator as a bigot and preached acceptance of those that were different than us.

Different than who, Clovis had asked Raylene when discussing the article. We're all different, he had told her. Plus, we're all a product of our upbringing, our environment. Our indoctrination, he had said, repeating something the infamous Thinking Lincoln had once told him.

Clovis got out of his cruiser and stretched his aching joints. His leg was aching like mad as he limped closer to the charred remains of the town limit sign.

Glancing up and down the road, he couldn't see any homes from this vantage point. The closest house was beyond a patch of forest which meant they wouldn't have seen the fire. The smoke wouldn't have been visible at 1 AM, which is about the time the arson should have taken place.

He thought the route over, from his home to here. There were no businesses with surveillance cameras that would be useful.

Dwayne had seen him and Raylene in their truck when he drove into work. Dwayne had waved at them in passing, so he had an officer of his own police force as a witness to them being parked at the festive Musgrave house, early that evening.

Then they had stumbled upon the accident in front of the church, which meant he also had the mayor and the town bad boy, Garth Blackett as witnesses to them being in town together. And they had all heard him, the chief of police, tell his wife to go home. He had asked her to make tea for him and Officer Adams.

This left a very small window of time where his wife could have driven out to this very spot, set the sign on fire, and return home to make tea.

Clovis smiled at the memory of getting home that night to find Raylene in the kitchen, herbal tea made for them and coffee for Dwayne. He recalled the fierceness in the way she had hugged him, as if they hadn't seen each other for a week. Plus, she had warmed up some chocolate chip cookies too; which Dwayne had thought she had just baked. Neither Clovis nor Raylene had corrected him on this so he would think she had been home, baking cookies and making hot drinks.

His wife had the perfect alibi.

Credible witnesses.

But Clovis knew it had to have been her that did it. He also knew that under the circumstances, she was going to get away with it too. A lump formed in his throat; his emotions welled up quickly at the thought that his wife had done this for him. His wife who had not an ounce of evil in her. His wife, who never even did anything remotely illegal or bad in her life, had committed a crime.

Clovis smiled and wiped away a tear.

"Maybe now you'll finally be able to let that go," his wife had said in reply when he told her what he had found. Not, I wonder who did it? Or I wonder if it was the same person who vandalized the crosswalk? Her concern had been solely about him. How this would affect him.

Still smiling, he called his wife.

"So how about a coffee, Mrs. McPhee?" he said to his wife when she answered the call.

"Finger sandwiches?" she asked in reply.

He could hear the smile in her voice, and it made his heart feel as if it might burst.

"That would be lovely," he replied. "But I wouldn't want to trouble you."

"Oh, it's no trouble, Chief McPhee."

"I'll be home soon," Clovis replied as he ended the call.

He holstered the phone and limped back to his cruiser while wondering if he should let her keep the secret or tell her he knew. He was sure there was nothing linking her to the arson. No proof that is, he thought as he drove home with an ache in his heart, a tear in his eye, and a smile on his lips.

Part 10

More

40

AT NINETY-THREE-YEARS-OLD, Eli Woodman didn't have the strength to walk his property anymore. Something he had done into his mid-eighties. So, when wandering his expansive property became too much, Eli accumulated parts from his multiple old Case L Tractors and got one running. He used the tractor as an excuse to keep gardening a while longer, even if the garden got smaller and smaller each passing year. Ernie eventually convinced him to give up the garden in exchange for free groceries, delivered of course.

But at ninety-three-years-old, the days were long with no garden to keep him busy. So, Eli wandered his property on his Frankensteined tractor. Wearing an old plaid jacket over his undershirt to protect him against what he thought of as a cool breeze, he drove out to a wild blueberry patch to check their progress. He was saddened by the abundance as he couldn't pick them anymore. The last time he did, it took the better part of an hour for him to be able to get his aching joints up off the ground again.

He drove on a beaten path out to his apple trees. Eli had planted scores of apple trees long ago. The nearby raspberry bushes looked like they would have a bountiful harvest again this year. The wild strawberries plants hadn't done well for the last four years but they looked much better this year. It bothered him that he could no longer reap the bounty nature provided without help. His aging body simply wouldn't let him harvest any of it anymore. Perhaps he could call his son again, like he had taken to doing the last few years. Ernie would bring his wife and a few others to collect some of the bounty, half of which they could keep. An arrangement that Eli had grown quite fond of since it often meant fresh pies, made and delivered. He was grateful for their help, but he longed for the days when he could fend for himself. He longed for the days when he harvested it all himself. He longed for the days when his wife made the best pies, God rest her soul, he thought.

He steered up a beaten path that would take him past one of his old barns and back towards his house. It wasn't much of a path, just a set of tire tracks indented into the green grass by his tractor.

A sudden fierce urge to pee too powerful to ignore made Eli stop his tractor on a small slope. He eased himself off the tractor, stumbled off the side so that he wouldn't pee directly on the little wild patch of blueberries he stood next to. The hot urine splashed on the ground before the pain kicked in. His prostate was probably infected again. The pain intensified and his knees got weak, making his head swim. Dizziness made Eli swoon as he finished urinating.

He would call his son when he got to the house and ask him to make an appointment with his doctor. The pain had started a few days ago but had gotten remarkably worse in such a short amount of time.

A bout of weakness made Eli drop to his knees, drenched in sweat as he blinked away tears in his eyes. As the pain subsided, he breathed deeply and cursed himself for getting so old. If this is what his life was now, better for the good Lord to take him and be done with it, he thought.

He spat on the ground and took a deep breath. He patted down his wild wispy hair with his arthritic hands and breathed deeply. As he did so, Eli spotted something blue in the patch of brush in front of him.

"Som-bitch," Eli muttered as he struggled to his feet, joints popping loudly in the process. He didn't bother with the dirt and grass stains on the knees of his dirty dark brown slacks. He pulled himself onto his old tractor and steered it off the path towards the brush. The tractor sunk slightly in the field, but it had little trouble making it to the spot he had noticed.

He stopped the tractor next to the brush and lowered himself off gently, afraid of another bout of prostate pain.

He wasn't surprised by what he found on the other side of the brush. The mound of garbage bags, many of which clearly had been torn open by wildlife and spread out, had been there a while. Many of the bags and their contents were blanched by exposure to the elements. These had been there for a long time. Probably years. Although part of the pile was new. The blue and clear transparent bags and their contents recently placed here evident by their lack of discoloration compared to the rest of it.

"Som-bitch," Eli muttered, running his hands through his wispy hair.

The old stuff he could have accepted. It had probably been put there before he ever knew it was happening. But the batch of new bags were recent. So recent that they hadn't been discovered by wildlife yet. Which meant they were dumped here since his visit to his neighbor about this very subject.

He hadn't learned a thing. That som-bitch had dumped more trash, thought Eli.

41

A FRUSTRATED JACK LEDGER sat in his white rental SUV, across the street from Ms. Musgrave's overly festive house. He held his cellphone to his ear, waiting.

"Hello," he heard as the call was answered.

"She's gone too far!" Jack stated firmly, skipping any sort of formal greeting. "She put one of those stupid inflatable things in her yard."

"Jack?" he heard Bonnie Campbell ask.

"And there's no point in calling Clovis. He won't do anything about it."

"Of course not," Bonnie replied.

Jack cut her off and continued ranting.

"The lights I could handle but now she added more. More tacky garbage. It's July, for Pete's sake. Almost August."

"So what?" Bonnie replied.

"So? We're almost August and she's adding more Christmas decorations!"

"Leave her alone, Jack. Stop being a bully."

Jack started to reply but realized Bonnie had hung up on him.

"It's a damned conspiracy," Jack muttered as he watched a FedEx truck turn onto the street and come to a stop in front of Ms. Musgrave's house. The driver hopped out of the truck and disappeared behind it.

"More?" Jack said aloud. "You've got to be shitting me?"

He watched as the FedEx deliveryman reappeared from behind the truck, carrying a couple of brown boxes. Jack sighed as he watched him walk towards the festive home with what could only be more stupid Christmas decorations.

A smiling Ms. Musgrave emerged from her front door to greet the deliveryman. She signed paperwork with a flourish as they chatted, most likely about her festive display, thought Jack.

"He must think she's crazy," Jack muttered.

The deliveryman paused on the way back to his truck to take a picture of the festive home. Smiling, he pocketed the phone, climbed in his truck and drove off.

Looking towards the house, Jack saw Ms. Musgrave standing at her door, waving at him.

Embarrassed, Jack drove off while thinking about slashing a hole in that inflatable Christmas tree with the elves; wondering if he could get away with it.

42

"HELLO?" REGGIE SAID AS he walked up to the empty police bullpen of the Carlton police station. Nobody was at any of the desks. He carried a couple of takeout Santorene coffees.

"Libby? You in the shitter?"

"I'm in here," Libby said loudly. "In the Chief's office."

"Don't let the chief catch you in here, snooping around," Reggie said as he set a coffee cup on the desk near the computer mouse Libby was moving around.

"Har-har," Libby replied as she scooped up the coffee and sat back. "Clovis asked me to download the pictures from his phone to his computer earlier. I'm sorting them into folders for him so it's not as overwhelming."

"He seems tired, lately," Reggie stated as he sat in the first chair facing the desk, his knees almost as high as the top of the desk. Reggie made the chair look like children's furniture.

"I know, but it's to be expected, considering."

Reggie sipped coffee, shifted in the chair as he spoke. "I can't help but wonder how Raylene is doing."

"She's frazzled; I can tell you that much. But she's trying to keep it together as much as she can," Libby stated as she sipped coffee. "For Clovis."

"Is their daughter back from Paris yet?"

"Anna? She should be by now."

"I figured she wasn't back yet since we hadn't heard anything," Reggie said as he got up, pausing at the office door. "Anyway. I'm going back out there."

"Okay then," Libby replied as she woke the computer from sleep mode, typed in a password and got back to the task of sorting the hundreds of pictures Clovis had on his phone.

She created a folder for pictures of the defaced rainbow crosswalk.

She created a folder for the pictures of the town limit sign. Turned out Clovis' obsession with said sign was worse than she thought. Clovis had taken a lot of pictures of the sign, both before and after someone burned it.

She created a folder for Jack Ledger and Garth Blackett's accident in front of the church. The mayor's car looked worse than she had thought, but the pictures of Garth's rugged truck looked like it barely had a scratch. Dwayne had told her all about it, but until now, she hadn't seen the damage for herself. She zoomed in on the pictures of the truck and saw scratches and gouges on part of the metal bumper. But Garth wouldn't be angry about those. Heck, he'd probably be proud of them, thought Libby.

And lastly, she made a folder for Clovis' personal pictures. There were a lot of happy selfies with his wife. Quite a few of them posing in front of Ms. Musgrave's decorated house. She felt strange looking at some of these pictures as they felt like a peek into her boss's private life. A private life she felt he deserved, especially with everything they were going through.

Libby wiped away a tear as she copied all the folders to a shared drive she could access from her computer. Chief Clovis hadn't asked her to do this but it felt right. Considering the circumstances and all, thought Libby as she wiped away a fresh tear and sipped coffee while thinking she didn't know how much more of this she could handle.

Part 11

Wedding?

43

ANNA GOT HOME ON A Saturday, locked herself in her old room and cried for an entire day. When she eventually emerged she was red eyed and completely disheveled. A complete mess. Her first question had seemed selfish, but her parents had expected it.

In grade three, Anna had decided she would marry little Harvey Willet. He was a year younger than she was but already stood six inches taller than her. He was especially kind and she loved him for it. She had decided she would marry him as soon as they were old enough. That way her father could give her away at her wedding. Something she had dreamed of until her teen years saw her become focused more on making her parents proud instead of childlike fantasies. But those fantasies had never truly gone away for Anna. Secretly she still wanted the man she adored to give her away at her wedding, more than anything in the world.

"Who's going to give me away at my wedding?" she had asked before bursting into sobs.

It didn't matter that Anna had broken up with her boyfriend and therefore was in no way close to getting married. But now her father's cancer had returned and this time, there was no hope. It was simply a matter of time, and time was fleeting.

44

Sitting upright, propped up on a colorful plethora of different sized pillows gathered from all over the house, Clovis sat in the middle of their newly purchased Queen-sized bed. On his right side, snuggled up was his wife, Raylene. On his left, with her head resting on his dampened shoulder was his daughter, who at this moment, looked like a small child again.

"This reminds me of the time you fell off the monkey bars at school," Clovis said as he palmed away a tear, reminiscing about when Anna was ten.

"We don't call them monkey bars anymore," Raylene stated, her impulse to teach people the politically correct terms to use getting the best of her. Although she often used the antiquated term as well, only she tried not to in front of the children.

Clovis smiled and kissed his wife on the forehead.

"I hated having my leg in a cast," Anna replied. "But I loved the attention you guys gave me afterwards."

Anna smiled sheepishly and reached for a fresh tissue and blew her nose loudly. She balled up the tissue and tossed it at the small wicker trashcan next to the hamper. The ball of emotion-filled tissue bounced off the wall and landed on the floor with the others they had tossed previously.

Clovis guffawed. "Oh, I remember. You made us watch *The Lion King* seven times in one day."

"Eight," quipped Raylene.

"It wasn't eight," Anna said looking at her father's reaction. "Was it?"

Raylene smiled as she spoke. "You didn't want to eat anything other than mint chocolate chip ice-cream and potato chips."

"I was a kid."

"You still are," Clovis said, wrapping an arm around each of the women in his life and hugging them.

"So, are you okay?" Raylene asked her daughter.

"No," Anna replied bluntly. "But this is not about me."

"No, it isn't," Raylene replied. "But you're our little girl, no matter how old you get."

"My father's dying," Anna said, her voice cracking with emotion, a fresh tear running down her cheek.

"Yes. I am," Clovis replied. "But I've made my peace with it. Also, I'm not dead yet."

Raylene clasped her daughters' hand in hers.

"Does Cotton know?" Anna asked.

"Your brother is off being the best he can be," Raylene replied solemnly.

"Your brother is overseas somewhere right now," Clovis added. "I've contacted his commanding officer and filled him in on what is happening. But I asked him not to tell him yet. But he'll be home soon enough. Don't worry."

"Good," Anna replied as she took another tissue and dabbed at her tear-streaked cheeks.

"I was looking forward to having him meet your boyfriend," Clovis said with a smile.

Raylene poked a stiff finger in her husband's chest. "Shush!"

"Is it true about Ms. Musgrave?" Anna asked.

Raylene smiled wide and hugged her husband.

"She's an angel, that woman," Clovis stated.

"At first I would have said the same," Raylene interjected. "But the more it pissed off Jack Ledger, the more she delights in it. I'm thinking for a sweet old lady, she has some devil in her."

"They're just Christmas decorations," Clovis quipped.

"Not to the Mayor they're not," Raylene replied as she yawned.

"There's mint chocolate chip ice-cream in the freezer," Clovis said as he hugged his daughter. "And I got something for us to watch."

"I once swore I'd never watch *The Lion King* ever again," Raylene said with a knowing smile. "Now I can't think of anything I'd rather watch."

"I'll get the ice-cream," Anna said she crawled out of

bed and headed downstairs.

"It's like she's a kid again," Clovis said as he started to get up, before being pushed down by his wife who kissed him on the cheek. She got up and set up the Blu-ray for them to relive a cherished memory, just like they talked about doing under the glow of Ms. Musgrave's festive lights.

45

WHILE SITTING IN HER home office, concentrating on her writing, Bonnie Campbell was startled by her ringing phone. She hit save on the article before reaching for her cellphone. She smiled as she answered the call.

"Hey sailor. Looking for a hookup on a Sunday afternoon, are we?"

"What have you been telling people?" Jack Ledger asked abruptly.

"What do you mean?" Bonnie asked, her playful mood dissipating quickly.

"I bumped into Ms. Musgrave and Ernie Woodman at the grocery store."

"So?"

"So, Ernie asked me when the wedding was?"

"Wedding? What are you talking about, Jack?"

"You and me! They wanted to know when we were getting married. Can you believe that?"

Bonnie burst into laughter.

"It's not funny, Bonnie. What will people think?"

"Who cares," Bonnie replied, still tittering.

"But I'm a widower, and the mayor too."

"So?"

"Good thing my wife is dead. This would just about kill her."

Bonnie's smile vanished and her brow furrowed as she spoke.

"If your wife wasn't dead, Jack; we wouldn't be fooling around now, would we?"

Bonnie listened for a reply, but none came. She knew Jack was bewildered and not thinking straight. Clearly, he was bothered by what people thought of him. This wasn't a secret. The entire town knew this about the mayor.

"It's not like we're doing anything wrong, Jack. Naughty, sure but not wrong."

"But you used to work for me. I sold you the newspaper."

"So?"

"People talk, you know."

"Are you ashamed of being with me, Jack?"

"Yes."

"What?"

"No, I mean… I'm the mayor and my wife is dead."

"Keep talking Jack because right now I'm not happy."

Bonnie felt a sudden strong urge to have a drink. Something she hadn't had in the last few days.

"You know what I mean, Bonnie. At our age. What kind of example are we setting for our kids? For the young people of this town. What will they think?"

"Who cares?" Bonnie replied. "Maybe now you can take me out to dinner."

"In public?" Jack asked.

Shocked, Bonnie ended the call abruptly, set the phone down and glanced at her desk drawer, wishing she still had a bottle stashed in there.

Her phone rang as she swiftly hit ignore.

The phone rang again.

"What, Jack, what?"

"I didn't mean it that way," Jack muttered in what Bonnie knew constituted an apology from the proud Jack Ledger.

"I guess I wasn't ready for people to know about us, is all I'm saying."

"We couldn't keep it a secret forever, Jack."

"I wonder how they found out?" Jack asked.

Bonnie knew this was his way of asking if she did tell someone.

"Jack. How many times has your car been parked in my driveway? Especially at odd hours."

"True," Jack replied in a subdued tone.

Bonnie often marveled at how a man like Jack, a successful man, could be so blissfully unaware. Especially since he made it his business to know all about the goings-on in their little community.

"Now you are going to have to take me out to dinner. Today. Come pick me up. Goodbye!" Bonnie stated, abruptly ending the call.

"If you know what's good for you," she said aloud, wishing she would have said this to Jack before ending the call.

Part 12

He Knows

46

TROUBLE CAME NATURALLY TO GARTH Blackett, and it often found him at his place of employment. So, when equipment breakdowns caused them to fall behind schedule, Garth saw an opportunity to get on his foreman's good side. Plus, he wanted to outshine his coworkers as well, so he was the first to volunteer for overtime to help get back on schedule. It was full dark by the time Garth headed for home, that Monday night.

Garth slowed his truck to a crawl as he pulled into his driveway, his headlights catching movement in the shadows, near his front stoop. He stopped the truck near the road, at the beginning of his driveway and angled the headlights towards his dark house.

"Fuck," Garth muttered as he saw a large black patch move. Chills ran up his spine and gooseflesh coursed over his dirty forearms.

A pair of yellowish-orange glowing eyes turned towards the truck. The large black bear ignored Garth and turned its attention to whatever had previously drawn it out of the dark woods.

Garth flicked on his high beams and saw the bear was pawing at something on the ground before it. Eating.

In that moment, a second slightly smaller black bear appeared on the right and climbed his stoop. Once at the top, in front of the door, the bear scratched at something on the deck floor. The smaller bear bit at something and sat upright with what looked like a mauled box in its mouth. Not just any box, Garth realized. A Skipper Jack's Pizza box.

He knows, thought Garth.

Eli must have found all the other trash he had dumped on the old man's property over the years.

The smaller bear tore the box completely open and spilled pizza everywhere, which the bear quickly devoured.

The larger bear sniffed at the ground, looking for more food as it fearlessly wandered towards Garth's truck.

Furious, Garth punched the horn on his truck for a quick loud blast, startling the large black bear. It quickly turned tail and disappeared into the darkness.

The smaller black bear hadn't budged. It licked at the stoop, getting all the crumbs in the process.

Garth punched the horn a second time.

The smaller bear was unfazed as it slowly climbed down the stoop, sniffed at the air before walking slowly in the direction the larger bear had gone.

Eli knows, thought Garth as he climbed out of his truck. The headlights still on, he paused near the open door, ready to jump right back in again if the bears came out of the shadows. He listened, hesitated, but nothing came. He turned off the lights and slammed the truck door, hoping to scare any more nearby bears. Once on the stoop, Garth examined the mangled Skipper Jack's Pizza box.

A sudden shuffling noise from the woods made the hair on his neck stand up as he struggled with his front door. Once inside, he slammed his fist into the drywall next to the door frame, leaving yet another indentation in the shape of his knuckles in the battered wall.

47

HER LIVING ROOM LIT with a small lamp and the faint glow of a laptop; Libby sat on her couch wearing her favorite pajamas and clutching a glass of red wine. Libby sipped the wine and grimaced.

"Gah... why?" Libby muttered as she set the glass down on the coffee table. With a few quick clicks of her computer, she messaged her chat buddy and coworker, Reggie.

"I don't get the thrill of wine."

"Give it a chance," Reggie replied. "It grows on you."

Libby picked up the glass, sniffed at the wine and grimaced. She set the glass down on the coffee table again and typed a reply.

"I'm not so sure about that."

"Trust me," Reggie replied.

Libby looked at the wine and thought about what Reggie had said earlier that day. Have it with cheese first to cut the bitterness. Libby went to the kitchen to get cheese but had a change of heart on her way to there. She grabbed a beer from the fridge, cracked it open and drank half while standing before the fridge.

Libby belched.

"So ladylike, right Odessa?" Libby said as the stray cat she had recently adopted came out from her bedroom and sauntered to the couch. The large black cat sat on the floor and looked at Libby as if waiting. Libby sat on the couch with her laptop again, beer in hand instead of wine. The cat hopped onto the couch and climbed behind Libby to lay on the back of the couch. It gently placed a paw on Libby shoulder and began to purr.

Libby gave the cat a scratch under its chin and returned to the task at hand. Sorting the rest of the images she had downloaded from Chief Clovis's cellphone. She had previously sorted most of the images by what they pertained to.

She had a folder for the defaced rainbow crosswalk. There were pictures of the vandalism itself, including a few pictures of Father Finnigan's feet as Clovis hadn't deleted his accidental images. There were pictures of a lid that had to have been from the paint can used in the act of vandalism. Evidence, she thought. What did Clovis do with it, she wondered. She knew he had taken it with him, but he hadn't mentioned anything about it since.

A few mouse clicks later and she was in a folder for the burnt village limit sign. She knew full well about the Chief's obsession with the sign, so she wasn't exactly surprised to find pictures of it before it was burnt. Libby clicked back and forth between the images, thinking about the time they debated simply painting it themselves, but eventually deciding against the idea. She recalled something about it being a matter of principle to the chief.

She examined the pictures of the burnt sign while recalling how Clovis had grinned foolishly when he told her about it. He had relished the fact that the town council no longer had a choice but to replace it.

Smiling at the thought, she proceeded to the folder of the accident in front of the church. She marveled at the pictures of Garth's truck. It being an old work truck to begin with, she couldn't tell if it had sustained any damage from the fender bender itself or if it had been like that from previous roughhousing. However, the mayor's car should be a write off, she figured. The trunk lid was crumpled like an accordion, folded against the back window. Both back fenders severely buckled, the mangled bumper pushed down and skewed. The difference between the amount of damage to Garth's truck and the mayor's sedan was unbelievable.

A few more clicks brought her to a folder of Mrs. Musgrave's house covered with festive decorations which clashed with the dandelions on her lush green lawn. There were close-ups of brightly lit decorations. A few of the pictures were selfies of the chief and his wife during their late-night visits to the festive home.

Libby felt a tear run down her cheek as she looked at a selfie of Clovis and Raylene posing with Mrs. Musgrave, everyone smiling wide.

There was also a folder of personal pictures which

Libby felt she shouldn't be looking at but couldn't help herself. Clovis and Raylene at the lake. Clovis and Raylene having a picnic in a field somewhere. Clovis and Raylene snuggled in bed or in his truck.

The pictures Clovis had taken of Raylene felt personal. Raylene cooking, cutting the lawn, but the picture of her sleeping was too much for Libby. Her emotions were getting the best of her, she closed the folder, and chugged the rest of her beer. She wiped the tears from her eyes and scratched the cat behind its ear, making it purr.

"Oh shit," Libby muttered as she opened a folder again and went searching for the picture she now recalled seeing earlier. She paused on one image, zooming in.

"Oh shit! He knows," Libby said as she closed the laptop, grabbed the wine and drank it as fast as she could to avoid tasting it. She set the glass down and ran to the bathroom and vomited.

48

"WELL HELLO SAILOR," BONNIE said as she heard the front door open and close. Jack had let himself in with the key she had given him. She adjusted her negligee, fixed her hair, smiled and propped herself at her bedroom door, leaning against the jam.

"Why don't you come into port, sailor?" Bonnie began before pausing, confused by the expression on Jack's face.

"Jack? What's wrong?"

Jack took off his jacket, the same one he always wore even on a warm July evening such as this. He flung it on the couch, which Bonnie saw as uncharacteristic for the mayor who always hung his coat on the hooks near the door.

"I drove past the Musgrave house on the way here," Jack stated as he slipped out of his shoes and undid his pants while still standing at the front door.

Again, so uncharacteristic of him to do this. Bonnie stiffened as she spoke, her relaxed mood slipping away.

"You need to let that go before you have a heart attack."

"That's not the point," Jack said as he dropped his pants next to the couch, making the contents of his pockets jingle.

"Jack! If you have a stroke, we won't be able to keep doing this," Bonnie replied.

"I saw Clovis and Raylene parked up the street."

"Ah!" Bonnie exclaimed.

"They were cuddle up like kids in his truck," Jack said.

"They do that often, Jack," Bonnie stated in a matter-of-fact tone.

"Really?"

"Yes, really."

Bonnie went to the kitchen to pour herself some red wine but recalled not having any when standing before the open fridge door. She took out the cranberry juice and poured a little in a pair of tumblers.

"I mean they were just sitting there, like a couple of kids, in the truck staring at the Christmas lights."

"You do know Clovis's cancer came back, right?"

Still in his socks, underwear and shirt, Jack sat on a kitchen stool behind the island, his shoulders slumped.

"Yeah," he muttered. "I know. But he's going to beat it again. Like last time."

Bonnie set the tumbler of juice before Jack and sipped at her own.

"Not this time, Jack."

"You can't know that," Jack replied as he picked up the glass and stared at the dark liquid.

"I do, Jack. Clovis and I have the same doctor, and he told me so."

Jack looked up from his glass which he had yet to drink from.

"No way. Doctor patient confidentiality. There's no way he spoke to you about Clovis without his permission."

"Well, he didn't exactly tell me right out, but I asked, and I could tell what the answer was."

"You could tell? Seriously?"

"Yes, Jack. I'm a reporter. I'm good at reading people."

Jack sank his glass and coughed, gasping.

"Is this juice?"

"Cranberry. You do know Clovis isn't going to see next Christmas, don't you?" Bonnie asked, wanting to change the subject from the contents of the tumbler back to their previous conversation.

"But he looks good. Other than the limp, he looks pretty healthy."

"He's lost his edge, Jack. I can see it. It shows in his lack of interest in his work."

"That would explain why he's not done anything about those stupid Christmas decorations at the Musgrave house."

Bonnie's face flushed with frustration.

"After all this, you still don't get it?"

"Get what?" Jack asked looking at his empty glass.

Bonnie exhaled loudly and poured more cranberry juice as she spoke.

"He won't live to see next Christmas, Jack."

Bonnie sipped juice to give Jack a moment to reflect on what she had just said.

"They met at Christmas time," Bonnie added. "It's their favorite holiday for a reason, Jack."

Jack lifted his glass to take a sip and paused, his glass hovering before his face. Bonnie saw his expression change. Finally, she thought. He's clued in. It would have been a lot easier had she not promised Raylene to keep this secret. Raylene had reached out to Bonnie, concerned that she would write something in the paper. For good reason too, as Bonnie had considered doing exactly that. Although she had been drunk when she started writing the article. And when Raylene asked that the paper respect their privacy, Bonnie had understood what she was really asking. That Bonnie herself refrain from putting anything in the paper. At least while Clovis was still alive, that was. This is what a drunken Bonnie had replied to the wife of a man dying of cancer. The next day,

Bonnie quit drinking.

Bonnie watched Jack sink the cranberry juice. He grimaced at the sweet and sour taste and when he put the glass down, his expression had changed. Now he knows. He finally knows why Mrs. Musgrave started lighting her Christmas decorations again. Why her festive home was still brightly lit in the warm evenings in July.

Bonnie drank her juice, wishing it was wine.

"You look nice," Jack said with a sudden twinkle in his eye.

"Let's go to bed," Bonnie said as her lips curled into a sultry smile.

Part 13

Bygones be Bygones

49

Two days later, early in the morning, Jack had driven his rental SUV to Mrs. Musgrave's house with nothing but good intentions. Now that he knew the reason behind the festive decorations, his bitterness towards the little old lady had subsided enough for rational thinking to kick in. Not only was he willing to let bygones be bygones, but he was also going to give her some money to help pay for the cost of the electricity. He had learned from a few on the town council that people had been collecting money for Mrs. Musgrave, and he felt he couldn't let himself be outdone. Although he had been quite vocal about his disapproval, so writing a check was out of the question. This would be proof that he could admit to being wrong. Cash would be better. It would make it easier to stretch the truth if needed. And so, with a couple of crisp hundred-dollar bills in an envelope, Jack had driven out with every intention of swallowing his pride for a change. But that was before he saw what had happened since his last visit.

He climbed out of his SUV and stood in the center of the road in front of the Musgrave house. The number of decorations on the little old lady's house alone made him cringe. But now he marveled at the houses on each side as they had joined in the Christmas in July celebrations. The house to the left had a large inflatable display of Santa Clause in his sled with a pair of chubby cartoonish reindeer standing at the forefront. There was also a set of mini lights strung along the deck railing.

The house to the right had a large inflatable nutcracker standing in the center of the lawn. Near it were large homemade candy canes and multicolored lights were strung along the entire edge of the roof.

"Seriously?" Jack muttered when he noticed the house on the other side of that one had Christmas lights on the pair of cedar bushes that flanked the house.

Now there were four houses in total with decorations. Blood boiling in rage, Jack tore the envelope containing the cheque in half.

But then he remembered deciding not to write a check.

He had used cash instead.

The envelope in his hand had contained two hundred-dollar bills. Bills which he had just torn in half.

"Oh, for Pete's sake," Jack muttered as he climbed into his rental and drove off, hoping nobody had seen him.

50

It didn't happen often but occasionally Garth Blackett came to the realization that he was simply being an asshole. So, on his way home from a day's work at the cranberry fields, he had decided that he would stop dumping trash on Eli Woodman's property. Something he had done on and off, for the last five years. But he would stop. The incident with the pizza boxes and bears on his property had angered him greatly but it had also made him realize that maybe he deserved it.

The old man had never done anything to deserve Garth's disdain. He lived next door and kept to himself. Sure, Garth was jealous of the expanse of land the old man owned but that wasn't his fault. Garth had bought what was for sale, all those years ago. An acre and half of brushwood thicket, evergreens and part of a swamp. He kept waiting for the old man to die, so he could buy the land from Ernie. But it seemed like the old man would live forever, he often thought.

Now his poor decision to dump trash on the very land he wanted to purchase had come back to haunt him and regret was setting in. While at work, the idea of collecting the last batch of trash he had dumped on old Eli's property occurred to him. Perhaps he should go get it before the old man found it.

And maybe he should try and win favor with Ernie. As the old man's only child, he was sure to inherit the land. Garth was counting on the fact that Ernie wasn't the outdoor type. He wasn't the type of man who would benefit from owning such an expansive property.

Ernie lived a quiet life, ran a grocery store and already owned a house. Ernie wouldn't have use for his father's property, once the old man did finally die. So, while driving home after a long day at the cranberry beds, he had finally decided he would start trying not to rile up the old man anymore. He would clean up the trash he had last dumped. And he would try to be nice to Ernie, next time he saw him. He wouldn't kiss his ass or anything, thought Garth. Hell no. But he would be civil. Perhaps even respectful, if he felt Ernie deserved it that is. It would make buying the land a little easier when the time finally came.

But thoughts of being almost kind to Ernie and his old man dissipated quickly when Garth pulled into his driveway and saw a trash heap protruding from behind his house.

Garth killed the engine, slammed the door of the truck and marched behind his house to find another pile of trash having been returned to its rightful owner.

"Fuck!" Garth uttered in frustration as he kicked a large empty jug of motor oil across the backyard, making it ricochet off an old pine tree.

This pile was larger than the previous, with a blend of older sun-bleached trash and newer deposits as well.

Old Eli had found more of Garth's dumping grounds.

Sudden movement in the trash pile startled Garth and made gooseflesh course up his forearms. He took a few quick steps backwards.

From under the trash, a raccoon darted out and disappeared into the trees.

"Fuck," Garth muttered. Now what was he supposed to do this time? It had taken three trips to clean out the last trash pile and there was probably twice the amount this time. Garth nudged another grimy empty jug of motor oil as an idea crossed his mind on how to clean up this mess once and for all.

51

CLOVIS PARKED THE POLICE cruiser in his driveway, having just gotten home, and took his phone out of his breast pocket to check the missed call. It was his old friend Winston, who owned the Pinewood Lodge, where Clovis used to regularly play darts.

Winston had been on the town council going on two years now.

Clovis hung up on Winston a few moments into the call. After the brief exchange, Clovis had no desire to continue their conversation, not after the insinuation made by Winston.

What did he know about the town limit sign being burned, Winston had inquired. Clovis hadn't liked his tone of voice either.

The phone rang again. Clovis answered the call.

"What?" he blurted.

"I'm sorry," Winston interjected. "But put yourself in my shoes."

"You're kidding me, right?" Clovis asked incredulously.

"Look at it from our perspective," Winston muttered. "You used to be very good at that, looking at things from all perspectives."

"You think because I was after the town council for all these years to replace the city limit sign that I, the chief of police, set the damn thing on fire myself?"

"Well with your cancer being back and all, we figured..."

"YOU FIGURED WHAT?"

Winston sighed.

"That since... you know, your cancer came back, and you wanted to see the sign replaced before..." Winston trailed on.

"Before I die," Clovis replied before Winston could continue. "The town council thinks I burned the sign so that it would finally get replaced before I die."

Clovis swallowed hard, trying not to get emotional at the thought of his wife, setting the sign ablaze for that exact reason. Now the town council had enlisted Winston, who was friends with Clovis, to approach him about the idea. It wasn't like they could go to the police with this ludicrous theory. He was the police. And they weren't asking if his wife had burned the sign but if he had. Maybe this wasn't such a bad idea, he suddenly thought. Let them think I did it.

Clearing his throat, Clovis took a deep breath and spoke calmly.

"What does it matter who burned it?"

There was a pause before Winston replied.

"Well, we're thinking someone needs to be held accountable?"

"You do?"

"With the crosswalk being vandalized and now the sign being burnt, we can't not do anything."

"I suppose you're right about that," Clovis replied.

"How would that look? I mean if we did nothing. It would send a message that people can get away with that sort of thing."

"So does the council think the crosswalk and sign burning are linked?" Clovis asked Winston. His curiosity overpowering his irritation, helping him think clearly.

"Some members do but not me. And I'm not the only one. A lot of us feel these two things are probably not related but it's a small town and all."

"That it is," Clovis replied.

"Some think that it's probably just kids, up to no good."

"Some of the town council members are always happy to blame anything on kids. We got a lot of good kids in this town," Clovis stated firmly. It annoyed him that people always wanted to blame any mischief on kids. Most often it was ill-intentioned adults. Although not always. In the case of the town limit sign being burned, the intentions were as pure as they could be. Clovis cleared his throat and spoke.

"Well, you can tell them that maybe I did burn it... or not. You guys decide. Me? I'm tired. I'm hungry. I haven't eaten all day, and my wife is waiting for me to come inside."

"Tell Raylene I said hi," Winston replied.

"I will," Clovis stated. "And if you guys really think I burned that sign, you should call Libby. Goodbye, Winston."

"No hard feelings?" Clovis heard Winston say as he ended the call without replying, pocketing the phone. He thought about what he had just said about calling Libby. He couldn't help it. His cop instincts had kicked in when he said that. Under normal circumstances, they were right. If nothing was done about the burnt sign or the crosswalk, then people would get restless. They'd wonder what was next. Third time's the charm, some would say.

But that could wait. His wife and daughter were waiting on him to have supper.

Part 14

That Was Close

52

BEING OLD SUCKS, THOUGHT MS. Musgrave, but the alternative sucked even more. Nothing was more humiliating than a grown woman, peeing the bed, she mused as she pulled off her adult diaper, rolled it up and stuffed it into the small trashcan next to the bathroom vanity. At least if she was losing her mind and didn't know better, then she wouldn't be as embarrassed at the checkout counter while buying these damned things.

There was a time when the urge woke her so she could make it to the bathroom but that was then. These days, she was lucky if she woke at all. It was easier just to put on a diaper than wash the bedding every damned day.

Too tired to fuss, in the glow of her Christmas lights through the thin sheer curtain of her bathroom window, she cleaned herself quickly with a damp hand towel and slipped on a clean diaper. She slipped back into her nightdress, happy to be dry again.

On the way back to bed, Ms. Musgrave paused at her living room bay window and glanced towards the neighbor's house. They had put up new lights on a cedar bush and she had yet to see them lit.

"Oh my," she marveled.

The lights had a beautiful blue hue to them that would reflect off the snow in the wintertime, she thought. But even in this warm July weather, they shone a heavenly blue onto everything their light touched.

It made her heart smile that her neighbors were getting in on the act, putting up their own decorations. This is what she was thinking when a flickering caught her attention. A light suddenly went dim at the house next to her. She glanced at the house to her left and saw something was missing.

Sliding her bare feet into a pair of shoes by the door, she boldly went outside, feeling the cool air through her thin nightgown. The house to the left had had a large inflatable display of Santa Clause in his sled with a pair of chubby cartoonish reindeer standing at the forefront but it was gone now. Or so she thought at first. Until she noticed it was still there, only it was no longer inflated or illuminated. In the glow of the other Christmas lights around it, she could see it looked crumpled on the ground. A flicker and the set of mini lights strung along the deck railing went dim.

Sudden bright lights came on, illuminating the entire front lawn of the neighboring house as Ms. Musgrave watched from her stoop. Adjusting her glasses, she saw a bulky figure dart clumsily across the lawn, towards the street.

A door opened next door and she heard a voice speak up.

"Jack?" she heard her neighbor exclaim. "Jack Leger!"

"Oh, my stars!" Ms. Musgrave exclaimed. "He's finally lost it."

"They went that way," she heard Jack shout.

"Who?" the neighbor asked.

"The kids. The ones who cut up your Christmas decoration."

"What kids?"

"Little pesky hoodlums, that's who. They rode away on their bikes. I think there were three, maybe four of them. They went that way!" Jack exclaimed pointing up the street before climbing into his rental SUV and driving off in the direction he had pointed towards.

"Oh, my stars," Ms. Musgrave whispered as she broke into a giggle. She knew there were no such kids. The thought of the mayor getting so worked up over the Christmas decorations that he would stoop this low made her smile as she went back to bed.

53

IN THE BOTTOM OF a newly dug cranberry bed, Garth Blackett stood stock still next to his excavator, concealed in the shadows. Looking up, he saw wispy clouds partially hiding the waning moon contributing to the dark of night. He glanced past the machine's bucket and saw Mark-what's-his-face, the night watchman walking back to his truck.

Fuck that was close, thought Garth. Had he shown up five minutes sooner, Garth would have gotten caught red-handed. Shifting a little to get a better vantage point, he watched as the security guard got in his truck.

"Go away," Garth whispered, his patience wearing thin.

It was difficult for Garth to be sure from this distance, but the guard looked to be making a call. For a moment, it looked like the glow of a cellphone in the cab of the truck. After a moment, the glow disappeared, and the engine roared to life. The headlights came on as the truck backed up and drove away.

Breathing a sigh of relief, Garth stepped out from hiding and walked along the edge of the cranberry bed until he reached a set of wood steps near the end. Hesitating while peaking over the edge of the pit, he judged the coast to be clear. Cautiously Garth walked back to his truck, which he had parked behind a bulldozer.

Garth climbed into his truck, stuck his keys in the ignition but before he turned them, bright lights suddenly blinded him. He raised a hand to block the blinding lights when he realized the lights were moving.

The security guard hadn't left after all.

The truck pulled up next to Garth's.

"What the hell are you doing here in the middle of the night?" the guard asked.

Garth recognized him but couldn't recall his last name. He had seen him around town. The son or nephew or something of some asshole he'd gone to school with. He couldn't recall in the moment. He was too tired to think straight and now he had to talk his way out of this. His job depended on it.

"I forgot my damned phone in my digger." Garth said. He held up his cellphone as evidence. "I couldn't find it anywhere and so I figured it must have fell out of my pocket."

"And it couldn't wait until morning?"

Garth felt his face flush. His patience fading fast but he knew he couldn't be rude or this would get him into trouble. If his trials and tribulations had taught him anything was that if he kept his cool, the situation wouldn't need to be brought up again.

"Could you?" Garth asked, forcing a smile. "Could you have waited until morning?"

The guard raised an eyebrow and shrugged.

"Bad enough I missed a call from my lady friend," Garth lied.

"If you put it that way," the guard replied.

"Plus, I can't afford to buy a new one," Garth lied again. He could afford a new one. The truth was that he was too cheap to get a new one. His old one worked just fine. But that wasn't the point.

"Well, I gotta get home and see if I can get a few more hours sleep," Garth added.

Garth rolled up his window, started his truck and drove off.

In his rearview mirror he could see the cab of the guard's truck glow faintly. He could only assume the guard was calling in to assure whoever was on the other end of that call that all was fine after all.

Garth sighed in relief as he headed home. That was close, he thought.

54

LIBBY SAT AT HER desk in the bullpen of the modest Carlton police station, sipping at her first coffee of the day. She clutched the mug with both hands as if afraid to drop it, pausing between sips, savoring the coffee.

Officer Dwayne Adams slept in his chair; legs crossed with his feet propped up on the desk. Lately he had taken to tilting his head to the side, a result of a recent chair upgrade. And while this habit was new, the spot of drool on his shirt, just below his chin, wasn't. And as usual, a book lay in his lap with a bookmark protruding from its pages.

She marveled at how Dwayne slept in such awkward positions and had never once complained of any discomfort. But in this moment, what struck her as bizarre was that she had seen Chief Clovis McPhee leaving the station as she arrived and yet Dwayne still slept.

He had waved to her as he limped to his truck and drove away. And having seen the chief leaving that early in the morning, she hadn't expected to find Dwayne still sleeping. It was out of character for the chief not to have woken Dwayne.

But here was sleeping beauty, snoring still after the chief had been in and out without incident.

Sure, the chief wasn't his usual self anymore. That Libby knew. And she hadn't been there to share the laugh so the chief wouldn't enjoy abruptly waking Dwayne as much. But he always woke Dwayne. He knew how much Dwayne enjoyed briefing him on the night's events, even when most nights, nothing happened.

Libby sipped coffee, set her mug down and logged into her computer. A sudden thought occurred as to why the chief may have wanted some time alone in the office. A few clicks and Libby was looking at the chief's pictures, the very images she had expected to find missing.

Befuddled, she scanned through the folders, expecting

to find something amiss.

Backtracking, she compared the chief's file size to her own and found a difference. The chief's file was smaller after all. But the pictures she assumed would have been deleted were still there. It didn't make sense why she had assumed that he would have deleted these pictures in particular. There was a time when Chief Clovis would do the right thing, without question. Even when the consequences were steep. But that was then. These days, he seemed more than happy to sweep something like this under the rug, thought Libby.

She compared all of the sub folders one by one until she found what she was looking for.

The chief's file folder containing the burnt town limit sign was smaller than her copy. A few clicks later and she realized that all but a few obscure images were left. Libby split her screen and opened both folders side by side. She scooped up her cup, sat back and pondered while sipping coffee.

This didn't make any sense to her. Clovis had become obsessed over the years. The longer it remained vandalized, the more he wanted it repainted or replaced. He had even offered to do it himself, but the town council refused to let him. And since they knew he wanted it done, there was no way to do it in secret, even if he wanted to.

Libby sipped coffee as she heard Dwayne stir.

"Go home, Dwayne," Libby said. "Maureen must be home by now."

She glanced over and saw Dwayne standing before his desk, book in his outstretched hand as he stretched and yawned.

"Clovis in yet?" Dwayne asked.

"Haven't seen him," Libby lied. It would be easier to ask the next question if she didn't tell Dwayne about the chief being in earlier.

"Dwayne, was Clovis at the scene of the accident with you the night Garth rear-ended the mayor's car?"

"Yeah. He showed up not long after I got there. Why do

you ask?"

"I was just thinking, that's the night the town limit sign was burned."

"True," Dwayne replied as he gathered his hat, book and keys and readied to head home.

"Did you guys see anything strange that night? Maybe someone drove by at some point."

"Not really."

"You didn't see any other cars while you were out patrolling?"

"Nothing abnormal, no. At least nothing I remember."

"Did you know why Clovis was out that late?"

"He and Raylene were parked by Ms. Musgrave's house, admiring the Christmas decorations."

"Then Raylene was with him," Libby stated.

"Yup."

"Garth drove his truck home that night?" Libby asked.

"Of course. You can't stop Garth once his mind's made up."

"Clovis let him?"

"Once the tow truck driver agreed that Garth's truck was fine, Clovis let him go home."

"Who gave Jack a ride home?" Libby asked, already knowing they drove the mayor home but wanting to keep the conversation going.

"We did. Clovis and I."

"Raylene, go home with Garth?" Libby asked, trying to assemble the pieces in her mind.

"She took Clovis's truck home. She made us chocolate chip cookies," Dwayne replied as he walked towards the exit.

"She had time to make you guys' cookies?"

"Well, we were there a while. Clovis got the tow truck guy to inspect Garth's truck to be sure it was good to go. Then we stayed while he hooked the tow truck to Jack's car, too. Once the road was cleared, we drove the mayor home."

"You didn't take him to Bonnie's place?" Libby asked

with a smirk.

"Why would we do that?" Dwayne asked.

Clueless as usual, thought Libby.

"Have a good sleep," Libby said to Dwayne. "Tell Maureen I said hi."

As Libby heard Dwayne's car pull away, her mind went over their conversation as the pieces fell into place. There was no way Clovis burned the town limit sign. *No way*, thought Libby. But Raylene on the other hand, could have. And she would have the perfect reason to do it too.

Her husband was dying. This would set his mind at ease, Libby thought. One less thing to obsess over while he tried to make the best of the time he had left.

She would have had to go home, get a fuel can, unless Clovis had one with him but Libby knew he wouldn't. So, home to get a gas can, drive out to the town limit sign, set it on fire and then drive home to bake cookies for her man. It didn't sound all that outrageous now that she thought about it.

Libby sipped coffee and thought about the axe in her Jeep. She had decided she would take an axe to the defaced sign and make sure they didn't have a choice to replace it. But someone had beat her to it. Burned the sign.

It had to be Raylene.

That was the only way to explain why the chief deleted the images and had stopped talking about it. He knew. He knew it was his wife who did it.

Libby thought about the axe in her Jeep.

That was close, Libby thought as she sipped coffee.

Part 15

Lay Off

55

***L*IBBY WAS SURPRISED TO SEE** the chief at this hour. It was almost four in the afternoon and Clovis had taken to going home early more and more. Ever since his daughter got home, he had been spending less and less time at the office. And he couldn't be blamed, considering the circumstances.

Libby had every intention of sitting down with him and having the talk. She would do so as soon as she could muster the courage. Which so far, hadn't happened.

Chief Clovis had a sour look about him and hadn't said a word as he walked past her desk and straight into his office. Libby knew something serious was up when Clovis closed his office door. Something he hardly ever did, unless he felt it was for the best, he had once confessed. But the irony was that if she rolled her chair near the blind covered window in the wall that separated the chief's office to the bullpen and was as quiet as a mouse, she could make out what the chief was saying on his calls. Especially when he was upset, and his voice was raised. And just as she suspected, the light on her fancy phone indicated that the chief was on a line.

She inched her chair backwards, cocked her head a little as if it would help her hear better, and absentmindedly held her breath while listening intently.

56

"JACK," CHIEF CLOVIS MCPHEE said firmly into the phone.

"What can I do for you?" the mayor replied.

"I heard a disturbing rumor today."

"Do tell?"

Clovis sighed, ran his shaky hand through his greying hair and leaned back into his chair as he continued.

"I heard some *kids* were tampering with Ms. Musgrave's Christmas decorations."

Clovis heard no reply and so pressed on.

"I heard *kids* were vandalizing her and her neighbor's decorations."

Still no reply on the other end of the call.

"I heard there was a witness who saw these... *kids*."

"Who's that?" Jack Ledger asked.

"You, Jack. You saw them. Chased them off, I'm told. Or did you forget?"

"Me?"

"You forgot already?"

Clovis heard shuffling on the other end of the call. Chances were what he was saying was starting to sink in.

He'd known Jack Ledger all his life and while he couldn't say he disliked him; he couldn't say he trusted him either. Jack found ways to make things about him. And if he didn't like something, he often found ways to manipulate things to his favor. Or in this case, manipulate them so that he would get his way. And it was obvious that he had wanted to stir the pot and got caught in the act.

Clovis sighed as he continued.

"According to Ms. Musgrave, those *kids*," Clovis said still emphasizing the noun, "well, they sabotaged some Christmas lights and an inflatable decoration on her neighbor's lawn."

"I, uh..."

"And she says that if you hadn't been there to chase them off, well who knows what else they would have done."

"Yeah, true enough," Clovis heard Jack mutter. It was obvious he was trying to think of something clever to add.

"So, when can I expect you?" Clovis asked.

"For?"

"To make a statement."

"About?"

Clovis couldn't help but wonder what Jack had been doing when he called. Jack wasn't the fastest, but he was normally sharper than this. Much sharper.

"The *kids* who you saw vandalizing the Christmas decorations."

"Oh, right."

"I need you to come and make a statement. You must have recognized them. I mean you're the mayor and all and you know just about everyone in this little slice of paradise."

"I didn't recognize them," Jack blurted.

"Seriously? But you know everyone in this town?"

"They had ski masks on."

"In July?" Clovis retorted.

"Yes."

"Both of them?"

"Yes."

"So, you didn't tell Ms. Musgrave that two of them were white and one was black?"

"I think that's what I said," Jack replied.

"But a moment ago you said both, as in two and now there's three of them."

"Well, I didn't say both, Clovis. You did. And I don't like your tone."

"My tone?" Clovis said as he glanced at the frosted glass of his office window and saw the silhouette that would be Libby as she listened in on his conversation.

"Yes," the mayor replied.

"Jack. Listen. I'm just trying to figure out how reliable of a witness you'll be when I catch these troublesome kids. I take this sort of thing very seriously. You don't fuck with little old ladies like Ms. Musgrave. Not in my town, you don't."

Clovis smiled. He could hear the mayor squirm when he used the words, my town.

"How many kids did you see? Were they tall, short, fat, skinny?"

"Can I ask you a question, Clovis?"

"Sure," Clovis replied, his smile fading at the mayor's sudden serious tone.

"Those Christmas lights. They really for you?"

"You'd have to ask Ms. Musgrave to be sure but if I was to hazard a guess, I would say yes. Why do you ask?"

"I didn't know," Jack replied.

"The cancer's back," Clovis stated. "A little over three years ago, the doctor gave me six months. But I beat it. I beat the cancer."

"I'm sorry," Jack replied.

"But not this time. This time there's no beating it. But to be honest, Jack. I think the Christmas decorations are more for Raylene than me. She's the one who has to live on. She's the one who has to survive her husband in a town where everything will remind her of me."

Clovis could hear sniffling on the line. As if the mayor was getting emotional as he listened.

"So, I think Ms. Musgrave wanted to give her something to cherish that she wouldn't see all the time. Special memories that she wouldn't be reminded of every damned day. So, I think it's for my wife, to be honest."

"I didn't know," Jack repeated.

"We all have our secrets," Clovis added. "Anyway, about those *kids*."

"I wouldn't be able to identify them. It was dark and all," Jack replied.

"Dark? With all those Christmas lights?"

"They ran before I could get a good look at them."

"Okay then. If you put it that way. But if you think of anything. Anything at all. You never know what could help me catch those pesky *kids*."

"I'll call you," Jack replied before ending the call.

Chief Clovis hung up the phone, scooped up his keys and limped out of his office.

"I'm going home," he said to Libby. "Call me if you need me."

57

Libby watched Chief Clovis leave before she picked up her cell phone and made a call.

"Libby?" she heard the voice on the other end say.

"Yes, Jack. It's me, Libby."

"I told Clovis I couldn't give a statement," Jack replied sounding frustrated.

"A what?"

"What's this about, Libby?"

"We need to talk, Jack. You and I."

"What about?"

"I'd rather not do it over the phone."

"Don't play games with me, Libby. I'm not in the mood so get to the point."

"Fine. But before I do, what did Clovis call you about?"

"You don't know?"

"Know what?"

"He didn't tell you?"

"Jack…. Don't bullshit me!"

"He was asking about the kids who vandalized the Christmas decorations at the Musgrave house. He wanted to know what I saw. If I could identify the kids who did it."

"Can you?"

"Like I told Clovis, it was dark, and they had masks on. I didn't get a good look."

"I see," Libby replied.

"Is that what you called me about?" Jack asked.

"No. Like I said, I'd rather not do this over the phone."

"Look, Libby. I don't know what's wrong but I'm busy, tired and not in the mood so like my dear old mother used to say, shit or get off the pot."

"Fine. I'm sending you two pictures. Give me a sec."

Libby quickly selected a pair of pictures from the files she had uploaded to her phone and sent them to the mayor of Carlton.

"Let me know when you get them," Libby told Jack.

She could hear rustling sounds.

"I didn't get anything," Jack began when she heard the phone chime, indicating the photos had come in.

"Hello?" Libby asked.

The call either dropped or Jack hung up, she thought while glancing at the phone.

The phone rang, startling Libby and causing her to fumble the phone, nearly dropping it. She picked up the incoming call and put the phone to her ear.

"What do you want?" she heard Jack ask.

"For now, lay off Ms. Musgrave."

"Does Clovis know?"

"Honestly, I think so. Maybe, but I'm really not sure."

"Did you ask him?" Jack inquired in what Libby thought was a remarkably calm tone, considering.

"No. I don't want to bother him with this. He's got a lot more important things going on right now to deal with things like this. So, are we good?"

"We're good," Jack stated.

"Good!" Libby replied.

"Anything else?" Jack inquired.

"Nope."

"I gotta ask. Has anyone else seen these pictures?"

"Not yet," Libby replied.

"You haven't shown them to anyone?"

"No, Jack. I haven't. So, like I said, lay off Ms. Musgrave's Christmas decorations."

"Done," Jack replied.

"Good," Libby responded before ending the call.

58

JACK LEDGER'S PHONE RANG once more, startling him in the process. His first urge was to throw the phone as hard as he could into the brick fireplace mantel of his living room. The last two calls he had just taken had made his blood pressure rise to uncomfortable levels. Resisting the urge to smash the device, he sat in his recliner and glanced at the screen to see who was calling.

"What now," he muttered before answering the call.

"Hello," he snapped.

"Oh," he heard Bonnie Campbell utter. "You sound perturbed," she mused.

"Do I?" Jack muttered.

"What's the matter?"

"I'm not feeling well," Jack replied.

"I told you to lay off those butter tarts you love so much."

"It's not my stomach. Just having a rotten day."

"It wouldn't happen to have anything to do with those kids who you caught vandalizing Ms. Musgrave's Christmas decorations, would it?"

"Now what would make you ask that?" Jack asked bitterly. He could hear the amusement in Bonnie's voice. She was enjoying this, he thought.

"Rumors around town, is all."

"Rumors?"

"Word is, you stopped some kids from vandalizing Ms. Musgrave's Christmas decorations. She's telling everyone you're some sort of hero."

"I can't identify them. They were wearing masks."

"Oh. So, you think it was premeditated then. I mean if they thought to bring masks, they must have planned to do this."

"What are you talking about?" Jack asked.

"The kids. Unless they always keep masks handy for those times when the mood strikes them to commit crimes or something."

"Why are you asking me this?" Jack asked.

"Ms. Musgrave called me. She said I should write an article about how you stopped the kids from doing more damage."

"She what?"

"She even suggested a headline. 'Mayor saves Christmas in July!'"

"You can't be serious?" Jack replied. He could hear the smile on Bonnie. The joy in her voice. She was giddy and it pissed him off.

"It's genius, actually."

"You and I don't agree on what genius means," Jack barked.

"So can I get an official statement?" Bonnie asked.

"Like I told Clovis, I can't identify them as they had masks on."

"Clovis? You spoke to the chief about this?" Bonnie asked. "Did you call him, or did he call you?"

"What does that matter?"

"Well, if he called you, he could be investigating," Bonnie said.

Jack could hear a shift in her tone. Now she was more serious in the conversation.

"He's not investigating it," Jack said in a matter-of-fact tone, as if he knew for sure.

"Did he say that? Maybe I should call him," Bonnie said, now sounding very serious.

"Drop it, Bonnie."

"I can't. This is too good."

"You're not seriously considering writing an article about this, are you?" Jack asked.

"I think I might," Bonnie replied. "I mean I wanted to do a little fluff piece about Ms. Musgrave's Christmas decorations, but this adds a new twist. A different spin on it. And if I can get an inside scoop from our hero, well..."

"Lay off, Bonnie. It's not funny," Jack said as he ended the call.

Jack's phone blooped. He'd gotten a text message from Bonnie.

"Yes, it is!" the text read.

"Lay off," he texted in reply before tossing the phone onto the couch, out of reach.

Part 16

Smells Like Fish

59

WHEN HE FIRST STARTED, GARTH Blackett would have told you that working near home was great. It was a welcome change from always going away to work. While working in cranberry fields on the outskirts of his hometown, he could live at home and save money. Sure, most often housing and amenities were part of the deal but he always found himself spending money on ways to get away. Most often his new coworkers would end up not liking him. Most often this meant time alone where he would get bored, lonesome, and this would feed his aggressiveness and bad habits including drinking. The latter being a serious problem in dry work camps. So, working at home was a gift at first. But as usual, the gift soon soured. In the usual amount of time, his coworkers quickly tired of his boorish sense of humor and mannerisms. It wouldn't take long for even the outsiders to begin to dislike him. Soon he would be eating his lunches alone again. The one guy who carpooled with him quickly found himself another ride. So, it didn't take long for Garth to become cold and distant to his coworkers, with the one exception being his foreman. It wasn't easy but Garth tried to remain on his good side. There was talk of the job site expanding to double the original plans. This meant more work. So, Garth needed to stay on the foreman's good side, no matter what. Therefore, he tried hard not to lose his shit when he found more trash in the back of his truck, at the end of his shift.

At the end of a workday, standing next to his truck, he breathed deeply instead of doing what he really wanted to do which was shout. Shout at anyone nearby and demand they tell him who did this. Who put three trash bags in the back of his truck?

He saw a smiling Joshua walking to his vehicle.

Garth felt his anger rise and his face flush.

He'd overheard people calling him names like trash or the garbage man. This was probably a prank but by whom, he wondered.

"Hey Garth," he heard a voice say from across the parking lot. He turned to see his foreman calling out to him.

"What?" he barked, unable to quell the anger in his voice.

"Do me a favor will ya. Throw those trash bags in the dumpster at city hall for me on your way home."

Garth took a deep breath. So, it was him who put the trash in the truck. Breathing deeply, trying to remain calm and reminding himself he didn't want to get fired in his hometown, he bit his tongue and held back the torrent of curse words he would otherwise spew if it was anyone else.

"Some fucker ate fish two days in row," his supervisor remarked. "The lunchroom is starting to smell pretty bad."

And so, you threw the smelly garbage bags in MY TRUCK, thought Garth as he gripped the box of his truck. This wasn't going to help him get rid of his new slew of nicknames anytime soon. Resisting the urge to throw the bags at the supervisor's hatchback, he tossed his lunch into the cab and watched a smiling Joshua drive away.

"I'd take them with me, but I only have a hatchback. Plus, I've got nowhere to dispose of them," his foreman said. "And you have carte blanche to the dumpsters behind city hall."

The nicknames would surely stick after this bullshit, thought Garth.

Garth didn't reply. He tried not to look too pissed off and wasn't sure how well he was pulling it off.

"Thanks," the foreman added as he got into his car and drove off.

"Carte blanche. Pretentious prick!" Garth muttered as he drove towards town on his way toward Skipper Jacks for a box of pizza.

60

After supper, Ms. Musgrave opened all her windows wide. Her entire house smelled of fish, even her clothes. They smelled of bass to be exact. She had cooked it with lemon zest and spices, and it turned out delicious. But now her entire house smelled like fish. Her clothes were an easy fix as she changed into her nightgown earlier than usual. But the smell in the house had been a little more stubborn and the deodorant spray would make her wheeze. It was easier to open windows, even if she felt the breeze was cool for a July evening. Albeit she thought the breeze was always cool even when it wasn't for others. So, she had opened the windows.

And while at the window, she noticed the Christmas lights strung on her front stoop had come undone on the corner. In a pair of slippers, she went out to fix this. The hooks were still where they had been for the last ten years and so the wind must have made them come undone at some point, she figured. Once fixed, she examined her decorations, happy in what they meant to the people she held dear in her heart. Before she could go back inside, Ms. Musgrave noticed the string of lights hung on her gutters had come undone as well.

"Oh dear," she said, glancing up and down the street and seeing not a soul. It wasn't a hard fix. Just off the hooks, like the ones on the stoop, only not within easy reach.

Stubborn people often don't ask for help when they should, her neighbor will tell her about a week from now.

So instead of asking for help, she stubbornly marched out back and got the aluminum step ladder from her back deck and clumsily carried it around front. She propped it open under the dangling multicolored lights and put a foot on the first rung to test its stability. Finding it rickety, she moved it a little and repeated the test. Better, she thought.

She nervously stepped onto the first rung and stopped. It felt solid so she stepped up one more rung. It felt stable still. Gaining confidence, she climbed up two more rungs and reached up only to find the light still way out of reach.

It would be dark in a few hours and so she felt she couldn't leave the lights like this. Three more rungs and she could no longer hang on with her hands, but it still wasn't enough. One more rung and she felt the ladder sway under her weight. Her heart sank a little as she expected to fall and felt relieved that she hadn't. She paused on the last rung with only the top of the ladder left.

The lights now within reach, she tucked the lights onto the hooks again as vertigo kicked in and everything swayed briefly. Shaking, knees quivering Ms. Musgrave bent her knees until she could get a grip on the ladders' top. Stepping down a few rungs, Musgrave breathed a sigh of relief.

That's when she noticed part of the lights she had just fixed had come undone again.

"Poop!" she exclaimed.

She stepped up again and tucked the lights back in place, pausing to make sure they stayed put this time. And they did. They remained on the hooks, under the eve of the house.

Ms. Musgrave shifted her weight, and the ladder kicked out from under her. Before she realized what had happened, she was lying on the ground.

Dazed, she heard a voice. Someone was there.

Looking up, she saw the lights sitting on the hooks

where she put them just before her fall. She started to sit up and a jolt of searing pain shot through her, making her cry out.

"Don't move," she heard the voice say. "Call an ambulance," the voice instructed to someone.

In her confusion, Ms. Musgrave wasn't sure who had come to her rescue. What she did know is that she was in a lot of pain and her house probably still smelled like fish.

Part 17

When It Rains, It Pours

61

AT A LITTLE PAST 3AM, the sound of hard rain on his roof woke Garth. At first, he tried to ignore it and go back to sleep but a steady dripping sound caught his attention. The damned roof was leaking again, he realized.

The last time he was on his roof was four years ago, while his wife still shared his bed. She had nagged him constantly for years to fix the roof before it got worse, only she called it reminding him, he recalled. But instead of replacing all the roofing like she asked him to, he only replaced the damaged shingles and tarred the parts most needing it. It wasn't pretty but it worked. At least it had until tonight that is.

A rhythmic drip-drip-dripping sound came from the hall, just outside his bedroom, the same place it had been last time. Although the rhythm was much faster than he'd ever heard it before, but that was to be expected as this was more than a simple shower.

Staring at the ceiling, he wondered if it was raining this hard at the cranberry fields. If yes, they'd be too wet to work in, come morning. A day off, he wondered as he got out of bed. Wearing nothing but tattered plaid boxer shorts, he walked across the shadowy hallway to the closet next to the bathroom and got what he thought of as his wife's old floor washing bucket. In the barely illuminated hallway Garth was going to place the bucket under the drip, near the edge of the spare bedroom door. But before he could, he groggily stepped a bare foot in the puddle, slipped and fell hard, bashing his head on the floor.

His head throbbing and suddenly prone on the wet floor, he tasted blood. He quickly realized he had bit his tongue in the fall. Still clutching the bucket's handle in his right hand, Garth began scrambling to his feet, mad at himself for not turning on the light to see how much water there was. The room suddenly spun; a powerful feeling of lightheadedness made his legs feel like lead. He stopped in a kneeling position bracing himself against the doorway of the spare bedroom. With one hand, he pushed the bucket in the darkness, under where the drip should be. He stopped when he heard the sharp sound of the dripping water change to the dull hollow sound of it hitting the bottom of the bucket.

Feeling frustrated, wet and groggy, his head hurting and tongue swelling from the bite, he sat on the floor with his back against the open doorway. He took a deep breath, trying to calm himself while feeling the back of his throbbing head and checking his wet hand for blood but found only water. He touched his head again and found a tender lump. He probably shouldn't go back to sleep, he thought. Just in case he had given himself a concussion. That was the last thought that went through his head as the room faded to black.

62

MARK, THE NIGHT WATCHMAN from the cranberry site spent most nights watching porn on his phone, surfing online dating sites or stalking his ex-girlfriend. Some nights he did all three. In between his rounds, of course. Driving around the site in his truck, or walking, making sure all was well so he could get back to playing with his phone. But tonight, the reception on his phone disappeared and moments later, what felt like a tropical storm began. Torrential rain like he had never seen before. He started the truck and put the wipers on high, but they couldn't keep up. He couldn't see a thing and his phone had no reception.

After a good five minutes of the rain not letting up, he shut off the truck and checked his phone.

Nothing.

With still no reception on his phone, he tried the truck's radio and found only static.

Well, nobody would be foolish enough to cause mischief at the site in this rainstorm, Mark thought. So, reclining his seat, he closed his eyes and listened to the rain on the roof of his truck until he fell asleep.

63

THE SUDDEN QUIET WOKE the night watchman from deep sleep. Rubbing the sleep from his eyes, he noticed water still flowing heavily off his windshield, confirming the rain had just now stopped as suddenly as it had begun. Mark glanced at the time and assessed that the rain had lasted over two hours. Starting his truck, he was awestruck at the scene in the headlights. Deep puddles everywhere. The trees on his side looked as if they'd been shaken violently, causing them to shed a lot of their otherwise perfectly healthy leaves, which were strewn everywhere. The dark wet muddy ground was speckled with glistening dark green leaves.

He inched the truck forward, taking in the scene before him.

The weather channel had forecast potential showers, but they said nothing about tropical storms. This had the look of something you'd see off the coast when a storm blew by on the ocean. But Carlton was at least 30 miles away from the nearest beach.

The truck sank in mud as he drove around the perimeter of the newly dug cranberry beds. Panic struck as he felt the rear of the truck begin to slide sideways. Mark tried to speed up and steer the truck away, but it was too late.

The rear of the truck slid until the back wheels fell over the side and perched the truck with its nose in the air.

"Fuck," Mark uttered. He knew his boss would tease him about his stupid two-wheel drive Ford. You should have sprung for the four-wheel drive; he knew he'd say. He'd heard it a thousand times, but this would only make it worse.

"Faaaaaaaak..." Mark moaned as he felt the truck sliding backwards still. He quickly scrambled out and stepped away from the edge of the mushy pit and watched helplessly as the muddy side crumbled. The truck descended slowly in what looked like four feet of brown water at the bottom of the pit.

The truck seemed to float atop the dark water as it drifted away from the edge a little.

Mark patted his pockets.

"Fuck-fuck-fuck-fuck," he cursed. He'd left his cellphone in the truck. Lucky for him, he kept his small but powerful flashlight clipped to a belt loop on his jeans.

Flashlight in hand while walking back to the trailer, Mark marveled at the mayhem. In the moonlight he could tell all the newly built cranberry beds had four feet of water in them and a few looked to be crumbling at the edges.

As Mark trudged in the mud past one of the newly dug beds, he could see something shiny floating in the dark water. At first, he dismissed it as more leaves blown from the trees. But using his flashlight, he could see what looked like a silver beer can floating near the edge of the waterlogged cranberry bed. Next to that, his flashlight revealed a large white bottle of what Mark assumed was detergent. And near that was what looked like plastic bags and tin cans as well.

Mark skimmed the water with his flashlight and could see trash everywhere, all seemingly contained in this one cranberry bed. None of the other nearby beds seemed to contain much more than a few pieces of trash except for this one. Most likely those were pieces carried away in the wind and had come from this one bed. But it was in this bed that it all seemed to originate from. He could see more trash embedded in the soil on the end, where parts had crumbled away.

"What the fuck is this?" Mark questioned.

On his way back to the site office trailer, Mark slipped and fell flat on his back in the mud. By the time he made it back to the trailer, he was coated in mud and in the sourest of moods.

He called his boss and filled him in on the torrential rain and the impact it had on the newly built cranberry beds. The devastation. The crumbling beds full of water and the one mysteriously filled with trash.

Oh, and swallowing his pride, Mark told him about his truck sliding into one of the beds, only to listen to his boss guffaw.

Part 18

Rumors

64

IN NOTHING BUT HIS WORN plaid boxer shorts Garth woke, still wet and laying on the floor in the spare bedroom. The bright morning light coming from the window hurt his eyes as he unsuccessfully tried to rub away the grogginess.

There was a dripping sound coming from what was probably now a full bucket.

Trying to sit up, he realized just how sore he was. His back and hip ached as the memory of slipping and falling on his ass came back. His neck and shoulders were stiff from hours of laying on the floor. Plus, his head hurt which helped him recall the impact when he fell the night before. A painful groan reminded him that he had also bit his tongue in the fall.

Garth felt worse than if he'd gone on a drunk the night before. It took effort to get to his feet and shamble into the hallway.

Garth felt disheartened as not only was the bucket full, but it had overflowed. The amount of water was staggering. He gathered all his ratty bachelor towels from the hall closet, plus a few of the nicer ones his ex-wife had left behind and spread them on the floor in an attempt to soak up the water. When he realized that still wasn't enough, he took a few more dirty towels from the hamper and the one off the towel rack as well, adding those to the mix. His back aching throughout, he mopped up as much of the water as he could and draped the wet towels on the shower curtain rod, the towel rod, the hooks on the bathroom door, the doorknob and anywhere else he could get a purchase for one of the towels to hang dry.

In his bedroom, he stripped and draped his wet underwear to dry as well. He slipped on clean underwear and a wrinkled but clean t-shirt.

Garth cursed as he glanced at his alarm clock. It was past 9 AM and he really couldn't afford to screw up again, he thought. It wasn't like he had called in to say he'd be later either.

He'd tell them the truth; he thought while searching for his phone. But the more he thought about it, the more he realized truth was a bit ridiculous. He'd lied too many times for smaller things, insignificant events. And slipping on the wet floor during a deluge and knocking himself out would sound absurd. Plus, they'd laugh at him, whether they believe it or not.

That's right. The deluge, he thought as he found his phone on the floor between a trash can and nightstand. It must have fallen during the night at some point. More than likely, he knocked it off the nightstand while half asleep. But the deluge might also mean that the job site would be a mess and he may not be needed at work anyway. If they got this much rain as well, the ground would be too muddy and would need to dry after all that rain.

Panic struck when he saw 8 missed calls, all from his foreman.

There was a text too. *Call me,* is all it said.

"Fuck," Garth muttered as he found his cleanest pair of jeans and finished getting dressed.

Should he call his foreman or go into work and pretend he had lost his phone or something? Call and see what's up or wait, and see? Decisions like this were stressful for Garth, and if he stewed on them long enough, he'd work himself into some sort of trouble.

"I need a beer," Garth muttered, knowing full well that

was a bad idea.

His tongue was sore, his head hurt, his back ached, and his joints were stiff.

He'd get a coffee at the Santorene instead and go in to work. He'd tell them about his leaky roof. He'd tell them his phone got wet, and this is why he didn't call in. He couldn't call. He hadn't decided if he'd tell them about slipping and falling on his wet floor, yet. He could lie and tell them his alarm clock was his phone, and this is why he overslept, he thought as he rushed out the door and drove to the coffee shop.

By the time he got to the Santorene coffee shop, his plan was coming together nicely, he thought as he got in line inside.

"This place needs a drive through," he muttered to the unnaturally blonde sneering woman in line before him.

The blonde woman who wore a flower print blouse, turned her attention back to the cashier while paying for her order. The cashier pivoted and spoke loud enough so that Garth could hear the conversation.

"So yeah, they found trash buried in one of the cranberry beds last night," the cashier said to the woman. "I don't know if it was there all along or if someone put it there."

"Oh dear," the customer tittered, clearly enjoying the gossip.

Garth felt a wave of anxiety wash over him. The missed calls. The text. They must have been about that. But they wouldn't know it was him. Some might assume with the rumors of the troubles with his neighbor and all. And his new nickname of Trash Man wouldn't help either.

"Can I help you," he heard the cashier say, pulling him from his thoughts.

Garth ordered a large black coffee, paid and walked away without uttering another word.

With a quick glance over his shoulder as he exited, he saw another Santorene employee lean in and whisper something to the cashier. They were both looking in his direction.

That's when he knew he would forever be The Trash Man.

The woman in the flower print blouse looked directly at him as she pulled away in an older model minivan.

Garth slammed the door of his truck as he got in.

"Fuck," he muttered, noticing that the three trash bags the foreman had asked him to get rid of were still in the box of his truck.

"FUCK!" Garth shouted and slammed his palm into the steering wheel, before starting the truck and driving off.

65

Early that morning, Jack Ledger sat at Bonnie's kitchen table, reading a first draft of an article on her tablet.

"You can't be serious?" he asked without looking up from the device.

A few days before, a tour bus from out of town had detoured through Carlton just after dark and stopped at the Musgrave house. Bonnie had gotten wind that this might happen and had managed to get pictures.

In the picture, the tour bus had stopped in front of the Musgrave house while its passengers strolled up and down the street, taking selfies and group pictures in front of the festive homes.

"You thought the decorations would drive away tourists but instead it brought them," Bonnie quipped as she made coffee.

"Yeah, but they showed up after dark and left again without spending any money in town."

"We're not a tourist town, Jack. We never have been."

Jack grunted and kept reading.

"Are you trying to make me look like an idiot?" Jack asked after reading the part about the vandals seen by the mayor who claimed he couldn't identify them.

Bonnie giggled as she set a coffee cup in front of Jack

only to go back to the kitchen counter to fetch her phone after hearing the bing of a text message.

"If I didn't know any better, I'd think…" Jack began but was cut off mid-sentence.

"Oh poop!" Bonnie exclaimed.

"What?" Jack asked bitterly. "You're making me sound like…"

Bonnie interrupted Jack again.

"Ms. Musgrave fell and broke a hip!"

"What?" Jack asked, unsure if he'd misunderstood.

"Ms. Musgrave fell. She broke a hip according to my friend."

Jack sat speechless as Bonnie grabbed her purse and headed for the door.

"Where are you going?" Jack asked.

"To confirm the rumor. If it's true, I'm going to have to rewrite that article," Bonnie said as she closed the door behind her.

"Damn," Jack muttered just as he felt his own phone vibrate in his breast pocket.

66

"HELLO?" JACK SAID, ANSWERING the call.

"Have you heard about the cranberry site?" Jack heard his friend Winston inquire.

"What about it?"

"Garbage," Winston said, sounding excited.

"What?"

"They found garbage buried on the job site."

"Say that again?" Jack asked, unsure he had understood.

"Trash. They found trash buried in one of the cranberry beds. At first they thought it was old stuff from long ago but it's not," Jack heard Winston say.

"How would they know that?"

"The Santorene coffee cups have the new lids they got six months ago."

"You're a regular Sherlock Homes, aren't you?" Jack replied.

"Rumor is, Garth Blackett probably did it. He works there you know. And I heard people been calling him Trash Man or something, although I couldn't figure out why. Maybe this has something to do with it," Winston said. "Boy that was some rain we got last night, wasn't it?"

"What the hell! I gotta see this trash for myself," Jack muttered as he ended the call and headed out to the cranberry field to play mayor.

Part 19

Not Unlike a Norman Rockwell

67

ERNIE WOODMAN LIKED TO STOCK the grocery store shelves when he had time. As a manager, he felt doing this type of work made him look more approachable to the staff. To work on the floor with them instead of always being in his office or lording over them.

Today he mopped the floor in the back aisle in the ice-cream section. The roof hadn't leaked in over six years, since they last tarred the flat roof. But the previous night's deluge had revived an old leak near the air conditioning unit. And instead of getting the new kid to mop it up, Ernie figured he'd do it himself.

He'd heard about other places in town with leaky roofs from the previous night's rain. Quite a few homes and businesses alike, from the stories being spread around town. And he didn't have to wonder about his father's house. The roof leaked when they had light rain so there was no way it didn't leak with the previous night's torrential rains. And as soon as the store was taken care of, he'd drive out there and have a look for himself just how bad it was. Again, he'd try and convince his father that he should move in with him, regardless of what his wife had to say about it. His father's house was in such a state and wasn't worth fixing, in Ernie's mind.

That's what he was thinking about when he heard a clatter of what had to be cans hitting the floor. The sound was coming from the front of the store.

Mop still in hand, he found one of his employees helping an elderly man everyone knew as Mr. Brooks, pick up cans he had obviously dropped. The teenage cashier was reassuring the customer that it was okay. That it happened all the time and not just to old men with a wooden leg, the boy said with a warm smile.

Ernie smiled at this moment of kindness between one of his employees and a loyal customer. Ernie couldn't help but think this was like something from a Norman Rockwell painting. He loved seeing his staff, being so kind and helpful to customers. Especially to someone with a reputation of being crotchety like old man Brooks.

The boy placed all the cans on the conveyor belt for the elderly man and proceeded to help him load his heavier items on the conveyor.

All was well, thought Ernie as his gaze wandered through the large storefront windows to the sunny scene in the parking lot.

Under a bright blue patchy sky, in the parking lot stood the mayor. Jack Ledger was engrossed in conversation with a blonde woman in a flower print blouse. Ernie knew this was Beatrice, whom everyone called Bea for short. The conversation looked quite intense as both used a lot of hand gestures and had stern facial expressions.

Ernie leaned on his mop, wondering what they could possibly be discussing that could be so intense.

68

GARTH'S BLOOD BOILED AS he ruminated over what had just happened in the Santorene coffee shop. People were talking about him. And somehow, they knew that he was the one who buried the trash in the cranberry bed.

"Fuck," he muttered as he turned his truck around and headed towards town hall. Glancing in the rearview mirror, he could see the three trash bags his supervisor had asked him to toss into the town hall's dumpster. He needed to throw these into the dumpster and be rid of them as they sure wouldn't help him shed his new nickname. *Riding around town with fuckin' trash in the back of his truck wouldn't help anything*, thought Garth.

Slowing down as he drove past the grocery store, he saw the same familiar blonde woman in the flower print blouse, standing in the parking lot, talking to the mayor. In his side mirror, he saw them look in his direction as he drove past. He saw the mayor pointing towards his truck.

"I don't think so, asshole," Garth barked as he slammed the brakes of his truck, leaving skid marks in the process. He thrust the gear shifter into reverse and stomped on the gas. Swerving wildly, he managed to back the truck into the parking lot of the grocery store. In the rearview mirror he saw the panicked woman in the flower print blouse and the mayor scramble towards the doors of the grocery store.

"What?" Garth shouted as he climbed out of his truck. "You want to talk trash about me behind my back?"

He regretted his choice of words as soon as he finished saying them, which infuriated him even more.

In a blind rage, he took two bags of trash from the back of his truck and threw them at the woman's minivan. One bag bounced off and landed intact on the asphalt. The second bag burst open spraying smelly trash all over the side of the van and the parking lot.

Burning with rage, Garth scooped up the third bag which hooked on the side of the truck's box and tore open, spilling its contents at his feet. The smell of rotten fish was incredible. Garth kicked at the trash, casting a good portion of it in an arc across the parking lot.

That's when Garth noticed that not only the mayor and the flower print blouse woman were watching, but everyone inside the grocery store as well had gathered near the windows.

Ernie Woodman stood, mouth agape, a mop in hand, watching.

A young boy in a grocery store uniform had a cellphone and was filming.

'Fuck you all!" Garth screamed.

He climbed into his truck and left long skid marks as he sped off.

69

ERNIE WOODMAN CALMLY REACHED into his pocket, pulled out his cell phone and made a call.

"Clovis? I hate to bother you, but can you come down to the store. When you get a minute?"

Ernie paused, listening.

"Garth Blackett was here just now. Nobody's hurt or anything but I think you'd best come on down here as soon as possible."

Ernie listened.

"Let's just say Garth is expanding his trash spreading services to more than just my dad's place."

Ernie waved the mayor over as he spoke.

"Okay, thanks."

He ended the call as Jack Ledger approached.

"What was that about?" Ernie asked the mayor.

"Hell, I don't have the foggiest," Jack Ledger replied. "Did you call Clovis?"

"Just did," Ernie replied as he fumbled with his phone.

Should he call his father and warn him that an angry Garth might be coming his way? Or better yet, he should go and make sure his father was okay? Probably best to wait until Clovis showed up, Ernie thought. He couldn't leave the store, especially not with the parking lot now littered with trash. A few moments ago, he had envisioned the scene before him like something from a Norman Rockwell painting. The way he often envisioned life in this quaint little quiet town. Now it resembled something out of a bad made for TV movie. A movie where the town bad boy bullied everyone until the town's badass sheriff set him straight. But the problem was, the town sheriff, in this case, the chief of police, was dying from cancer. Ernie glanced at his phone, wondering if he shouldn't have called Libby instead.

"Fiddlesticks," Ernie muttered.

"What?" the mayor asked.

"Oh nothing," Ernie replied, pocketing his phone.

Part 20

Tired

70

CHIEF CLOVIS ENDED THE CALL as he sat next to Raylene on a wooden couch on his covered porch. He turned to his wife as he spoke.

"I gotta go. Something's come up."

"When are you going to give this up?" Raylene asked. "You know you can call Libby. I'm sure she's more than capable of handling whatever this is."

"It's Garth Blackett so I better do this myself." Clovis locked eyes with his wife.

"Why?" Raylene inquired. "Why do *you* have to do it?"

"You know why," Clovis replied while shifting his gaze to the dandelion speckled lawn which needed mowing again.

"No. Tell me," Raylene said as she leaned into her husband, laying her head on his shoulder. She clutched his arm and held it to her.

Clovis rested his hand on her leg as he spoke.

"It's Garth Blackett," Clovis stated sounding as if that should explain everything.

"You said that already. Is that supposed to mean anything?" Raylene sighed.

"Years ago, I had a chance to go after Garth, but I didn't so this is my fault."

"Is this about his wife?"

"I should have made her press charges."

"You know damned well she wasn't ever going to press charges against him."

"I should have tried harder."

"You respected her wishes. Like you always tell everyone else to do."

They sat there quietly for a moment, saying nothing. Clovis knew what his wife wanted. He had told her he would give this to her soon. But retiring would mean all he would have to do all day was dwell on the fact that he was dying. And he hated that she was right. He was simply getting too sick to keep doing the job.

"You don't have to retire today," Raylene said, breaking the silence.

It was as if she had read his mind, thought Clovis.

"But you're allowed to call in sick, you know. Especially since you are sick. And Libby can handle Garth Blackett. And if you're so worried she can't, then tell her to bring that lug Reggie with her."

A grunt caused by pain escaped him as Clovis wrapped his arm around his wife and hugged her close. With his other hand, he made a call.

"Libby. It's me, Clovis. Is Reggie with you?"

Clovis paused as he listened.

"Good. Listen. I need you to take care of something for me. I need you and Reggie to head over to Ernie's store. He's gone now but Garth Blackett strikes again."

Clovis smiled at his wife.

"You'll know what I mean when you get there."

Clovis pulled his wife tight to him as he continued.

"No. I won't be meeting you there. I'm tired. I'm not feeling well right now, so I need you to handle this for me. Can you do that?"

Clovis paused.

"Tell them I called in tired."

Clovis ended the call, slipped the phone into its holster and sunk into the bench a little as he held his wife.

"Thank you," Raylene stated.

71

WHILE STANDING IN THE trash littered parking lot of the grocery store, Mayor Jack Ledger watched the police cruiser pull up.

"Where's Clovis?" Jack inquired as the pair of officers exited their cruiser.

He spoke before Ernie had a chance to say anything. "Why isn't Clovis here yet?"

Officers Libby Terwilliger and her partner Reggie assessed the scene. There was trash scattered in the parking lot and a crookedly parked minivan looked to have been a casualty of the trash explosion.

The mayor looked like he had just won the lottery, beaming from excitement.

An anxious-looking Ernie stood next to the entrance of his store, watching customers come and go, profusely apologizing for the mess in the parking lot. He had a pair of garbage cans at hand, with a half dozen transparent trash bags protruding from his back pocket. Clutched in a tight grip was a pair of yellow rubber gloves.

"He called in tired," Officer Libby said to Jack as she pulled out a notepad and pen.

"Whose van is that?" Reggie asked.

"Beatrice's. She's inside," Ernie replied.

Libby spoke while jotting down notes.

"I take it she saw what happened?"

"We all did," Ernie replied while slipping on the yellow rubber gloves.

"Who's we?" Libby inquired.

"Mr. Brooks for one. Colin, my new cashier and I all saw it happen from inside the store. I'm not sure but I think Colin took video with his phone."

"I see," Libby stated as she jotted down notes.

"Bea and Jack were talking in the parking lot when it all happened. I'm not sure why but it's like Garth was targeting Bea specifically. It's all on the surveillance cameras. I can show you."

"That won't be necessary," Libby replied. "Not right now, anyway. But I will get you to email me the footage though." Libby handed Ernie business cards. "Get Colin to send me the video he took as well."

Ernie pocketed the cards as he spoke.

"Now I need to ask you guys for a favor."

"What's that?" Libby asked as she pocketed the notepad.

"I assume you're going out to Garth's place."

"You know I can't really discuss that but sure, let's say we are."

"Can you check on my dad? He's next door, as you're well aware. And with the history between Garth and him. I'm getting a bit tired of having to worry about my father living next door to that bully."

"Of course," Libby replied. "You call me right away if Garth come's around again."

"Sure," Ernie replied as he puffed open a new trash bag.

"Don't wait for him to do anything crazy. Call me right away."

"Understood," Ernie replied. "So can I pick this up now?"

"Yes. Of course. Right after I take a few quick pictures first," Libby replied as she pulled out her phone and began snapping pictures.

72

A SLOW DRIVE BY Eli Woodman's house revealed that all looked normal to Officers Libby and Reggie. Libby drove the cruiser slowly into Garth Blackett's driveway, expecting to find Garth's truck but instead saw the driveway empty.

"I wonder where he went off to?" Reggie asked.

Libby stopped the cruiser, scanning the property for any signs of life.

"You should call the cranberry site again," Libby said.

"No need," Reggie replied. "I told his foreman to call me if Garth showed up for work. Although he said he didn't think Garth would come in. Not today. Not after the trash they found buried in one of the cranberry beds."

"The what?" Libby inquired.

"You didn't hear? Last night's rains washed out some of the cranberry beds. Some of that rain exposed some trash someone had recently buried."

"You serious?"

"That's what I heard this morning while I was at the Santorene getting coffee."

"And you didn't tell me?" Libby asked.

"I was going to," Reggie replied. "Although by the time I was on my way to the station after you called, it slipped my mind."

"We were on our way to the grocery store where Garth had scattered trash everywhere and you didn't think to tell me about the trash at the site where he works?"

"Well, you actually didn't tell me why we were going to the grocery store. Only that we needed to go."

Libby knew Reggie had a point. And in actual fact, she hadn't known about the trash either until they'd gotten there. All Clovis had said was that Garth had struck again. That could have meant just about anything at this point. Garth was infamous for having a temper, something that had only gotten worse since his wife had left him.

"Should we check the house?" Reggie asked, grasping the door handle readying to exit the cruiser.

"His truck's not here and Garth doesn't strike me as someone who would take the time to hide that huge truck of his."

"True," Reggie replied, relaxing his grip on the door handle but nervously glancing about the property.

"So if he's not at his work and not at home, where could he be?" Libby voiced her thoughts aloud.

"Burnett's?" Reggie replied.

"It's too early for that," Libby stated.

"Garth doesn't strike me as someone who's against

day drinking."

"I meant it's not open yet. They only open at two now. Since they no longer serve lunch anymore."

"Drive around town? See if we spot him anywhere?" Reggie asked.

"Might as well," Libby replied as she turned the cruiser around in Garth's driveway. "But first we should really look in on Eli."

"You think Garth would do something to old Eli?" Reggie asked.

"In the heat of the moment, yes. If Eli had caught him dumping trash on his property, then yes. Eli forgets he's ninety-three. And I think Eli would have gotten angry too, which would then see Garth lose his temper."

"A recipe for disaster," Reggie stated as Libby drove the cruiser next door to Eli Woodman's dilapidated house.

73

"ELI MUST BE HOME," Reggie stated before pointing out Eli's Fargo, the only vehicle in the gravel driveway.

"I'm just glad his shotgun's still in the chief's office," Libby stated as she got out of the cruiser.

"Me too," Reggie replied, exiting the cruiser. "Although I don't think it could have been fired without exploding in the user's hands."

"I suppose that should make us feel a little better," Libby replied as she walked around Eli's Fargo and scanned the property for the old man. Reggie's considerable bulk made the deck sag and creak as he walked to the living room window and peeked inside.

"See anything?" Libby asked, while still scanning the yard.

Reggie cupped his hands to his face to better peer inside the old, dilapidated house.

"Nope," Reggie answered. "No sign of him. But he's ninety-four. He could be napping."

"Ninety-three," Libby replied.

"Should I knock?" Reggie asked as he stepped back from the window and glanced about, making the deck creak again. He marveled at the dilapidated condition of the house, the old white distressed hardboard siding, its crooked chimney, the rotting window frame and sagging decking.

"Maybe we should," Libby replied.

A sudden loud cracking sound startled Reggie and before he could react, gravity pulled him through the collapsing deck boards. Reggie fell backwards as the decking gave under his considerable bulk, wedging his legs in the newly created hole in the aged decking.

"Fuck!" Reggie shouted.

Libby, having heard the snapping of the wood, had glanced over to see Reggie gone from sight. She heard Reggie but couldn't see him. With a hand at the ready on her Taser, she stepped towards the house and saw the sight of her partner, crotch deep in the deck boards.

"Are you okay?" Libby asked.

"I think so," Reggie replied turning to Libby as she climbed the stairs. "Careful where you step."

Libby was smiling now.

"I see that," Libby replied.

Reggie could tell she was suppressing laughter.

Libby pulled her phone out and snapped a picture.

"Seriously?" Reggie snapped. "A little help here? If you're not too busy taking pictures."

Smiling, Libby took a few more pictures.

"I have to document this, in case you're injured," Libby started. "Since it's on the job and everything."

Reggie was wedged up to his crotch, both legs in a hole in the deck boards. His feet barely touching the ground under the deck, he tried unsuccessfully to push down with his hands to lift himself out of this predicament. The tired old deck boards he pressed down on sagged and creaked under the pressure of his efforts.

"Help me out of here, will ya," Reggie said impatiently.

Libby smiled and pocketed her phone then stepped

carefully on the sagging decking, walking where the structure still looked solid. Grasping wrists, she helped pull Reggie free from the creaking deck. Reggie managed to get into a seated position, his lower legs not yet out of the hole as he turned to Libby only to see parts of the chimney collapsing towards the both of them.

Seeing the look of shock on Reggie's face, she reached for her Taser as she spun around only to be struck in the face by a falling brick.

The sudden added weight of the largest piece of chimney caused part of the decking to come apart from the house and slide off its support blocks and slant away from the house. The deck boards under where Reggie sat gave way, at the same time pinning his legs under a part of the deck.

Reggie now trapped again, turned and saw Libby sprawled on the now slanted deck. Her face bloodied, she lay amidst pieces of the old chimney.

"Libby?" Reggie shouted at his partner, wondering if she was dead. She seemed to stir but probably was out cold.

That's when Reggie heard a rumbling sound. It sounded like an engine but too rough to be a car or a truck. He tried to look around and see where it was coming from but couldn't really see over the outdated bench rail on the side of the old deck.

Reggie managed to pull out both his gun and his phone and made a call.

"I need an ambulance at Eli Woodman's place, stat." Reggie wasted no time. "Libby's hurt and I don't know how bad. I'm stuck and can't get to her. Get here as fast as you can."

"Fuck," he muttered as he heard the rumbling engine getting louder. He twisted his body, trying to see where the noise was coming from as it suddenly stopped.

Part 21

The Predicaments

74

HAVING DRIVEN HIS OLD CASE L Tractor along the edge of his property on Short Fir Road, an overall clad Eli Woodman pulled into his driveway and immediately wondered why there was a police cruiser parked behind his Fargo. But he didn't have a chance to wonder on that long as the collapsed deck and crumbled chimney pulled his attention from the police car.

Eli parked the old tractor next to the police cruiser and killed the extremely loud engine.

"What in tarnation?" Eli muttered as he dismounted the old tractor, stiff joints popping and snapping in the process.

"Who's there? Identify yourself!" Eli heard someone shout.

The fact that the car sitting in his driveway was a police cruiser emboldened old Eli as he stepped up to the front of the collapsed deck. From this vantage point, he saw the big cop named Reggie waist deep in what looked to be a new hole in the deck floor.

"Som-bitch," Eli muttered, running his hands through his wispy white hair.

Grasping the stair rail, he began climbing the stairs but paused when Reggie yelled at him.

"No... don't come up here!" Reggie shouted. "It's not stable."

Eli paused, now seeing Libby as well. She was sprawled out on the deck amidst pieces of his collapsed chimney. She looked hurt.

"Som-bitch," Eli muttered again. He reached into a bulging pocket of his overalls and pulled out a huge grey flip phone and dialed the only number he knew by heart.

75

STANDING IN HER KITCHEN holding a cordless phone to her ear, Raylene watched her daughter Anna wash the morning's dishes while her husband now out of uniform and wearing a t-shirt and sweatpants, sat at the table sipping coffee.

"Okay, thank you for calling," Raylene said before ending the call.

"Who was that?" Clovis inquired.

"That was Bonnie. Ms. Musgrave asked her to call us."

"Oh?" Clovis said with a raised eyebrow and inquisitive tone.

"According to Bonnie, Ms. Musgrave is in the hospital. She fell and fractured a hip."

Anna paused, soapy plate in hand as she spoke.

"Is she the old lady with the Christmas lights you guys told me about?"

"Yes, she was good friends with your grandmother," Raylene replied as she put the cordless phone on its base and sat at the table by her husband. "Bonnie says she's fine but they're keeping her at the hospital for a day or two. She didn't want you to hear the gossip and wonder."

"Well, that's good," Clovis replied. "One less thing to worry about."

Raylene grasped her husband's free hand as she spoke. "According to Bonnie, she's going to be fine."

At that moment, Clovis's cellphone rang. A quick glance told him it was Ernie Woodman. Again. Clovis wasted no time in answering, earning himself a dirty look from both his wife and daughter.

"Ernie. Did Libby and Reggie not take care of everything?" Clovis asked before Ernie had had a chance to say anything.

"I just got the weirdest call from my dad," Clovis heard Ernie say.

Clovis locked eyes with his wife as he spoke.

"Whatever it is, I'm sure Libby can handle it."

"That's the problem. My dad called me to tell me that Reggie was stuck in his deck and that Libby broke his chimney."

"I'm sorry… what?" Clovis asked, assuming he misunderstood.

"Those were his words. And I'm not too sure what to think," Clovis heard Ernie state.

"Where are you now?" Clovis asked.

"I'm at the store. I had two call in sick this morning so I'm short staffed and can't leave just yet. I got someone coming in so I can go check on my father but I'm going a little crazy."

"I see," Clovis replied.

"I called the police station, and nobody answered. I tried Dwayne and got his voicemail. He's probably still sleeping since he works nights and all."

"Ernie, you're rambling," Clovis stated coldly. He looked over at his wife with despair as he knew she wouldn't be happy with what he was about to say.

"Look, Ernie. I'll make a few phone calls. Find out what's going on. There's no point in my going out half-cocked without knowing anything anyway."

Clovis ended the call and wasn't surprised to see the look of displeasure on his wife's face.

"I know I need to give this up. I know I'm too sick to keep doing this," Clovis stated. "But something happened. I need to know what, before I can decide if I need to go handle it or not."

Clovis dialed Libby's number. It rang four times and went to voicemail. He then dialed Reggie's number and was surprised to have his call answered right away.

"Talk to me, Reggie!"

"We're at Eli Woodman's house. The paramedics are here now. They went to get a chainsaw to cut up the deck. They used the jaws to pry up the deck so it wouldn't bear down on me."

"I don't understand what you're telling me, Reggie," Clovis stated.

Clovis noticed the look of displeasure on his wife and daughter had changed to looks of concern.

"The deck at Eli Woodman's house collapsed. I'm pinned under it. I don't think anything's broken but I'm trapped."

"Where's Libby?"

"She got smashed in the head by Eli's chimney. She's out of it. Mumbling something barely coherent about rainbows and paint."

"Is she okay?"

"The paramedic said he thinks so. Knocked out cold but he says she looks okay. Maybe a mild concussion but they're taking her to the hospital now."

"Eli must be pretty steamed with all this happening on his front stoop," Clovis replied.

"About Eli. Did you give him back his old shotgun?" Reggie asked.

"No. Ernie asked that I hang on to it for a while. That he'd pick it up. Why?"

"After Eli found us, he went around back. When he came out again, he had a shotgun when he left in his Fargo. This one looked newer, like in working order."

"You didn't stop him?" Clovis asked.

"I was pinned under the deck and Libby was out cold."

"Right," Clovis muttered. He knew that already. He had to admit to himself that he wasn't as sharp as he used to be. Everyone was right that it was time to retire. Although letting these kids take over didn't seem to be working out right now, he thought.

"You didn't tell him about Garth spreading trash at his son's grocery store, did you?" Clovis asked.

"No but I think Ernie may have slipped and said something to him."

"I'll call Dwayne to see if he can lend a hand."

"I got a hold of him a few minutes ago," Reggie replied. "He's out looking for Garth now."

"So is Eli," Clovis replied.

"I told Dwayne that too."

Clovis ended the call.

"I'll go with you," Raylene started to tell her sick husband.

"You know better than that," Clovis said angrily. "Just let me do this one last thing and then, I'll hang it up for good."

"Promise?" Raylene asked.

"Promise!" Clovis replied as he limped up the stairs to get into uniform one last time.

76

AT MID-AFTERNOON UNDER CLEAR blue skies, Mayor Jack Ledger parked his newly repaired silver sedan in Ms. Musgrave's driveway. He sat quietly examining the contrast of the Christmas decorations and the green, freshly cut lawn.

He stewed at what had just happened a half-hour ago. He had bumped into Bonnie at the Santorene coffee shop where in front of witnesses, she gave him a key to Ms. Musgrave's house, asking him to do her a favor. She had stated loudly that Ms. Musgrave had wanted him, the mayor, to go and turn on her Christmas lights. She wanted him to turn them on and leave them on until she would return home, in a few days, give or take.

Jack fumed at the predicament Bonnie had put him in. He knew Ms. Musgrave had asked no such thing of him. She wouldn't have trusted him. Not after he publicly made it known how much he didn't like the Christmas decorations being up in the midst of summer. But Bonnie had also known that he wouldn't be able to disparage the decorations if he was suddenly made responsible for them.

He couldn't very well campaign against allowing these to stay up if he was tasked with making sure they remained lit. Although now that he understood why the old fool kept putting up more decorations in the summer months, he didn't feel as resentful. Now that he understood she wasn't just doing it to spite him, he found himself much more willing to accept them. Especially since those tour buses were coming through town now, even though they weren't spending their money in the local shops and restaurants.

Stepping out of his sedan, he sighed at the thought of what he was about to do. He was about to go light up the entire house full of Christmas decorations he had spent months trying to get taken down.

Before Jack could take a step, he watched a police cruiser drive past.

Pulling his phone from his pocket, he called Chief Clovis.

"Was that you? Just now? Driving past Ms. Musgrave's house?" Jack asked.

"Yes. It was," Jack heard Clovis say.

"I thought you were sick?" Jack asked.

"I'm dying, Jack. Of course, I'm sick."

"That's not what I meant."

"Question is, what are you doing at the Musgrave house?" Jack heard Clovis ask.

Jack sighed. He had hoped nobody would see him, especially Clovis.

"Just doing a favor for a friend," Jack replied.

Jack heard Clovis guffaw. He wanted to be upset that Chief Clovis McPhee was amused by this and then reminded himself the man was dying. If this can cheer him up, then fine, he thought.

"It is kind of funny when you think about it," Jack admitted.

"That it is," Clovis confirmed.

"Find Garth Blackett?" Jack asked, only to realize the call had been disconnected.

Or had it? Perhaps Clovis had hung up on him when he asked a question he shouldn't have. Clovis used to toy with him at times like that. Egg him on. Tease him with bits of information without divulging any details. But Clovis had gotten increasingly bitter in the last six months, but who could blame him considering he no longer had time to waste on trivial things like entertaining the mayor's curiosity. Jack mulled all this over as he made another call once inside the Musgrave house.

"Hey, handsome," he heard a jovial Bonnie say as she picked up his call.

"Yeah-yeah. So where are these switches and plugs you told me about?"

He had been too upset to pay attention when she had given him the instructions the first time. Now he could hear the amusement in Bonnie's voice as she talked him through the seven light switches and plugs that needed to be connected to get it all lit.

Once outside, standing in the driveway, examining all the Christmas decorations, Jack found he felt a sense of fulfillment after all. A feeling he hadn't expected to have based on the predicament he'd found himself in.

The sound of a vehicle's engine coming to life caught his attention, pulling him from his thoughts. A neighbor's SUV was backing out of her driveway. Jack waved and smiled at the woman and child.

Jack got in his car while there were witnesses to see him do so. He wanted them to know he had been the one to turn on the decorations. He found himself wanting them to know what he had just done. This was the same reason he had left an envelope on the kitchen counter containing a check for 250 dollars. A check she would have to cash at the bank, where everyone would see who it had come from. Jack would work this predicament into something positive, even if it killed him, he thought, watching as the neighbor drove away.

Part 22

War Path

77

CHIEF CLOVIS SAT IN HIS cruiser, parked in Garth Blackett's driveway as he watched the sun disappear behind the trees. It was near dark and no sign of the Trash Man anywhere.

Clovis called his wife.

"Hey hun. Just wanted to tell you everything is fine, so you wouldn't worry."

"I'll always worry," Raylene replied. "You know that. But I appreciate you calling to tell me everything is fine though."

"I can't imagine Garth having left town," Clovis said. He'd called his wife to tell her he was okay so she wouldn't worry but he also called her to think out loud.

"Is Dwayne still looking for him too?"

"Yes. He is."

"He must be tired, having been up all day and all," Raylene said.

"He slept after work," Clovis stated. "Besides, he's probably hopped up on caffeine by now."

"Any news on Libby?"

"She's got a mild concussion. I asked them to keep her at the hospital to monitor her condition. She's too stubborn to follow doctor's orders on her own."

"Sounds familiar," Raylene replied.

"Reggie's banged up, but nothing's actually broken.

Doc said if he wasn't such a big guy, the weight might have made the injuries worse."

"If he wasn't so big, he might not have gone through the deck in the first place," Raylene quipped.

"True," Clovis admitted. "Anyway. I'm going to take one more drive through town and then go home for a spell."

"Good," Raylene replied.

"But first I need to check on Dwayne. I love you," Clovis said to his wife before ending the call and making another.

"Dwayne. Any news?" Clovis asked.

"Nothing yet. I've been to the cranberry site, to Burnett's and I was just about to drive over to his house again."

"Don't bother. That's where I'm at now. The door wasn't locked, so I checked the house and he's not here. But the good news is Eli's home again. I saw his truck there and the lights are on."

"Good. We'll deal with Garth first and pay a visit to Eli in the morning," Clovis heard Dwayne voice exactly what he had been thinking and this reassured him that they could perhaps handle this without him, eventually that is.

"Go home, Chief. Raylene must be worried about you. I'll take it from here and call you if I need you," Dwayne added.

"I'm doing just that," Clovis replied. "But be careful, Dwayne. I got a bad feeling this isn't going to end well."

"I feel the same," Dwayne reiterated.

"Call me if anything happens. I want to put this to bed before I retire," Clovis replied before realizing what he had just said. There was awkward silence for a moment before they ended the call.

Clovis sat, staring at his phone, knowing this would be his last days in uniform. The pain was increasing, and medication wasn't as effective as it used to be. He was finally able to face the facts now. He no longer had a choice in the matter. It was being decided for him and this made him angry. Perhaps it was good that he didn't run into Garth after all. His patience thin and in a weakened state, he may have done something he would have regretted, he thought.

78

Eli sipped rum from his old, battered tin cup, while pacing the worn linoleum in his house. His neighbor, Garth Blackett had strewn trash on his property multiple times. That had annoyed him to no end, and he'd taken action to make sure it wouldn't happen again. He had no patience for such foolishness. But now Garth had spread trash in the parking lot of his son's grocery store, and this was the last straw.

Angry, Eli sipped rum while he waited for his chance to confront Garth one more time, he thought as he paused at his kitchen sink, looking out the dirty window towards his neighbor's place.

The sun had set behind the trees and dusk approached quickly. This meant he might be able to catch a glimpse of lights through the trees, if Garth was home. And through a dirty kitchen window, he saw faint illumination that had to be headlights.

"Som-bitch," Eli whispered as he felt his truck keys through the fabric of his old worn dress pants.

79

One last drive down Short Fir Road, thought Clovis. Then he'd go home to his family. He was already far down the side road and so might as well make it past the camps at the end before turning back. And with the sun having set, going past that wouldn't be safe as the dirt road got too bad for a police cruiser. He had no desire to get jacked up on some rut made by off road vehicles, he thought.

He put the cruiser in gear and headed slowly down the road, keeping his eyes peeled for vehicles parked in obscure places.

Garth always ran away from his troubles, thought Clovis. But usually, he ran away to his hometown where he felt safe. This time, the troubles were in his hometown so really, he had nowhere to run to. Chances were good, Garth knew he'd need to calm down before someone tried to hold him accountable for his actions or he was liable to make it worse. He had dealt with men like Garth a lot in his law enforcement career.

Clovis knew Garth wasn't the smartest but he also wasn't stupid either. He was a hot head, plain and simple. Once his temper flared, he no longer thought rationally or of consequences. He'd want to prove himself tougher, smarter, better than anyone who stood in his way. Superior or sometimes simply good enough. But as usual, once he calmed down, he'd realize he screwed up. *He'd go into hiding*, thought Clovis as he drove slowly down the road, scanning for anything out of the ordinary.

Clovis drove his cruiser past the line where the pavement stopped, and the dirt road began. Here he drove slowly past a few small camps until the road became unfit for a car. Having seen nothing that he deemed suspicious, he turned around and headed back towards town. If nothing came up before then, he'd head this way again in the morning. This time with his truck so he could go further down the back roads, he thought.

But as he approached Eli Woodman's land again, he noticed what looked like displaced grass in the shallow ditch. Clovis stopped the cruiser and pointed his Maglite and saw a second patch of flattened grass. There were two, wide enough to be a set of tires, thought Clovis. The ditch wasn't that deep that a large truck couldn't drive through it. But the tree line wasn't far in either. He couldn't have driven far, Clovis thought.

Pulling the cruiser to the shoulder, Clovis pulled his phone and made a call.

"You home yet?" Dwayne asked as soon as he picked up.

"Not yet," Clovis replied. "I took a drive down Short Fir and found something I want to check out."

"I can be there in 20 minutes, tops," Clovis heard Dwayne say with excitement in his voice.

"It might be nothing," Clovis replied as he killed the engine and got out of the cruiser. He pointed his flashlight at what he now could see where in fact tire tracks.

"It could be Eli's tire tracks," Clovis stated, even though he doubted it.

Eli's Fargo had narrow tires compared to Garth's huge work truck. And Eli's old tractor would have huge back tires and so would have left more obvious tracks. Mind you it was dark, and he was assessing this via illumination from a Maglite.

"Get here as fast as you can but be careful," Clovis added. "This may be a wild goose chase."

Clovis ended the call, holstered his phone and pulled his gun. He realized then and there that if Garth got violent, he'd have to shoot him. Garth Blackett would have been a fierce opponent for hand-to-hand combat in his younger days, but being in his mid-fifties and weakened by cancer, he couldn't risk engaging the younger Garth. And feeling the need to justify why he needed a gun to protect himself while pursuing someone in the dark of night, in a field reinforced the idea that he needed to retire. Leave this to the younger officers, he reflected.

Twenty feet into the field, his flashlight reflected off the taillights of Garth's truck. Pausing, Clovis scanned the tree line with his Maglite and saw nothing. Odds were good Garth wasn't far off. Maybe he'd cut through Eli's property to get to his. But Garth didn't have a lot of land and only had a house and a few small sheds. Most of which Clovis had looked at quickly.

Had Garth been hiding at his house after all?

Clovis couldn't help but wonder as he limped on, pain coursing through his lower body.

He should wait for Dwayne; he thought as he heard an engine roar in the distance. A vehicle approached. But it didn't sound like a police cruiser. It had the sound of an older vehicle with a bad muffler.

Clovis watched as Eli's truck came to a screeching halt next to his cruiser. Flashing his Maglite towards the truck, he saw a disheveled, red-faced grimacing Eli at the wheel.

Eli shone an extremely bright spotlight into the field where Clovis stood, blinding him.

"Eli!" Clovis shouted holding up his gun hand up to shield his eyes. His vision now filled with spots of phantom lights as Eli's truck sped away again, disappearing down the road. Clovis limped up to the ditch, waiting. A few seconds later, the old Fargo zoomed past again in the direction it had previously come from only to veer off into a side trail, its taillights disappearing into the woods.

"Damn!" Clovis exclaimed in frustration. Eli knew these woods better than anybody. If anyone had a good idea where Garth would be hiding, it would be Eli, Clovis thought. Hurrying as much as the pain would allow, he limped towards Garth's truck. *Garth isn't the hiking type*, thought Clovis. *He wouldn't have gone far.*

Scanning the inside of the cab, he saw empty beer cans, a pizza box and other trash. Cleanliness was not Garth's strong suit, he noted as he scanned the near empty box of the truck as well. In the back of the box, wedged at the tailgate he saw a tent peg attached to a short piece of yellow nylon rope. Perhaps for a portable hiding place, Clovis wondered.

Flashing the Maglite, scanning the tall grass, he couldn't find any traces showing someone had been through here, even though he knew there had been. Scanning the tree line, he also saw nothing to indicate any obvious traces.

"Who the fuck am I kidding," Clovis muttered. "I'm no fucking Daniel Boone."

Clovis un-holstered his phone and called Dwayne.

"Where the hell are you?" Clovis demanded.

"Almost there," Dwayne replied.

"When you see my cruiser, slow down. You'll see a dirt path that looks like it was made by a tractor. See if you can drive down it," Clovis instructed as he continued to scan the tree line for some hint of a path.

"I see it now," Dwayne replied.

Clovis heard the cruiser's engine in the distance, not all that far from where he was.

"Eli just drove down that with his Fargo. I'm on the other side of it, in a clearing. I found Garth's truck."

"Reggie said Eli had a shotgun," Dwayne stated.

"That's what Reggie said so be careful. Eli looked like he was on a war path," Clovis stated. "Oh, and put your phone on vibrate."

Clovis ended the call just as he caught a glint off something that looked out of place. Grimacing from the pain, he limped into the tree line where he saw two crumpled silver beer cans, obviously empty. Not far from that, he saw a pile that looked like human waste. Garth took a shit in the woods. Talk about leaving a trail, he thought as he saw disturbed forest debris farther along.

Part 23

Who's There?

80

HIS MAGLITE OFF AND IN complete darkness, Clovis stood stock still, trying to hear anything that might help. In his left hand was his Maglite and, in his right, his Glock. He slowed his breathing and waited for his eyes to adjust to the darkness. The faint rustle of leaves in the breeze helped calm his nerves a little and slow his racing thoughts.

There are four of us in here, he thought.

Old Eli Woodman, who as far as he knew, was probably carrying a shotgun. Loaded with what? Slugs, buckshot or something else, remained to be seen. But he had looked like he was on a mission and not playing around. Unsure if that made him more or less dangerous, the man was ninety-three and half blind, Clovis recalled.

Officer Dwayne Adams was in here too, most likely with his gun drawn and the safety still on. Dwayne wouldn't remove the safety unless he felt sure he would need to shoot. Dwayne was a damned good cop, but he got excited when the pressure mounted and so he'd be a walking adrenaline rush right about now, Clovis dreaded.

And Garth Blackett. The human tinderbox. If he'd calmed down by now, he may just come along quietly when asked, if Chief Clovis did the asking. But if Dwayne or Eli found him first, things would get crazy real fast. Dwayne would probably try to control the situation, perhaps intimidate Garth which would only inflame said situation. Who knows what Eli would do if he found him first. And while he assumed Garth wasn't armed, he couldn't be certain.

And then there was the fourth one. Me, Clovis thought. A man who survived his first bout of colon cancer but wouldn't survive this second time. A man in a weakened state, now incapable of handling someone like Garth Blackett unless he resorted to simply shooting him. And what if I did? I'd be dead before being brought up on any kind of charges for shooting Garth. I don't have much longer, thought Clovis. I can feel it now. I shouldn't have come out here. But what if I hadn't? This wouldn't end well either way, but I need to be here to try and mitigate the situation, Clovis regretted.

81

His eyes now adjusted for the darkness, Clovis limped forward hoping he was right that Garth wouldn't have ventured far into the forest. And sure enough, he stepped on something that gave a crumpling sound. Even in the complete darkness, he could see the glint off the empty silver beer can at his feet.

That's when Clovis heard a belch.

"Garth?" Clovis said aloud. Trying not to be too loud, he continued. "Garth. It's me, Clovis. Chief of Police."

Another belch.

The sound of a beer can crumpling from somewhere in front but a little to the right. He heard what had to be the beer can being tossed away and bouncing off something hard and landing on the forest floor.

Clovis pointed his gun, taking his safety off. He poised the Maglite at the ready but didn't light it yet.

Listening intently, Clovis heard crackling twigs to his left. The sound was subtle. Like someone trying hard to be quiet. Clovis didn't think that at ninety-three, Eli would have the dexterity and stability to creep up so quietly. He also didn't think Dwayne could contain his adrenaline to remain that still either. Maybe a deer, Clovis hoped. Hopefully not someone armed and dangerous.

The sound of a beer can cracking open helped him narrow down the direction Garth should be in.

"Garth?"

"Fuck this town," Garth muttered. "Fuck this town and everyone in it."

Clovis heard a cracking sound coming from his left again, this time louder, followed by a sudden rustling sound of leaves on his right.

"Eli?" Clovis said loudly into the darkness, so the old man would hear him.

"Fuck him too," Garth barked. "Old greedy fucker has too much land and never wanted to sell me any. Probably gonna give it to that useless boy of his."

Clovis heard a loud crackle to his left, pointed his gun at the area and lit his Maglite blinding Dwayne in the process.

A glint of silver shone from where Garth sat and Clovis suddenly realized the others may not know this was a beer can in Garth's hand. They'd probably think Garth was armed.

Shuffling sounds from ahead, what sounded like a zipper and then water being poured on the ground? Or was that Garth having a piss, wondered Clovis.

Clovis spotted Garth with his Maglite.

Garth, who wore a denim jacket with a puffy vest over it, had his back to Clovis. He was emptying out his bladder.

In front of Garth, at a slant strung across multiple trees was a green tarp secured with yellow nylon ropes. Scattered beneath it were various pieces of what looked like camping gear.

What sounded like a loud stumble came from the dark on Clovis' right.

Clovis shifted his light to the sound and spotted Eli, stumbling about, shotgun in one hand. The old man straightened up, squinting. Eli flicked on his powerful flashlight and shone it at Clovis who reeled from its powerful blinding light.

Eli flashed the light around and spotted Garth zipping up his fly.

"Fucker," Garth said as he pivoted to face Eli.

"Som-bitch!" Eli exclaimed.

Clovis knew in that instant, the green tarp and the camping gear would look like trash to Eli. In the dark, the glint from the silver beer can would be a gun to the old half-blind man.

Behind the powerful flashlight, Clovis saw Eli shoulder the shotgun and aim towards Garth.

Without hesitation, Clovis aimed and fired, shooting Garth in a calf muscle causing him to scream and fall to his side.

Eli simultaneously dropped his flashlight and pulled the shotgun's trigger a second too late, missing the fallen Garth but not Dwayne.

The shot clipped Dwayne's left shoulder and arm with what he would later learn was birdshot, making him grunt and stagger, accidentally pulling the trigger of his own gun. But the gun didn't fire as the safety was still on.

Clovis aimed his Glock and Maglite at Eli to see the old man had already lowered his shotgun.

"Did I git-um?" Eli asked, his face flushed.

Clovis kept his Glock and Maglite trained on Eli as he limped over and took the shotgun from the old man who didn't resist.

"You alive, Dwayne?" Clovis asked without taking his eyes off Eli.

"Fucker, you shot me!" Garth shouted.

"Ah FUCK... he got me in shoulder," Dwayne replied, pulling out his own Maglite. He used it to check his wounded left shoulder and saw less blood than anticipated. He then proceeded to use the Maglite to look around, assessing the scene before him.

"I'm gonna lose my leg," Garth squealed. "I can't see... am I bleeding bad?"

"Call an ambulance," Clovis shouted at Dwayne while checking Eli's shotgun and finding it empty. "Call an ambulance and tell them we have two with gunshot wounds."

Chief Clovis took a step to the side and fell face forward in front of the flashlight Eli had dropped.

"Chief?" Dwayne screamed.

"What's wrong with him?" Eli asked.

"Never mind him, I've been fucking shot!" Garth lamented as he squirmed from the pain.

Dwayne pulled his phone from his pocket and called 911. He rushed to Clovis and turned him over and saw no gunshot wounds or anything else for that matter. Grunting from his own gunshot wound, Dwayne checked the chief and found a pulse.

"The Chief's down," Dwayne blurted at the 911 operator. "I don't know what's wrong with him. I mean I know he has cancer and all, but he just fell over. He's got a pulse though," Dwayne blurted in confusion.

"What's your location?" the operator asked.

"Up Short Fir Road," Dwayne blurted, followed by detailed instructions to where exactly they were. The operator assured him that help was on the way. Dwayne thanked her and ended the call.

"Shit! Fuck! Son of a...." Dwayne lamented as he called 911 again, not bothering to ask if he had the same operator.

"Oh, and I forgot. We also have two people with gunshot wounds," Dwayne stated, hearing murmurs on the other end of the line.

"Seriously?" Garth asked incredulously. "Oh, by the way, we got gunshot wounds too," Garth said mockingly mimicking Dwayne.

"Shut up!" Dwayne replied as he realized Eli was gone.

Dwayne checked Clovis for vitals again to be sure he really was still alive.

"Thank God!" Dwayne said aloud, feeling a pulse.

Part 24

What Happened?

82

A PLAIN CLOTHED OFFICER LIBBY stood in the quiet hallway of Stonevalley Hospital, looking at the closed door of room 305. In this room was a father figure she greatly admired. Devastated, she had cried the first time she found out Chief Clovis McPhee had colon cancer. This second time she had felt numb. It was as if she had accepted losing him the first time, he fought the disease. But he had survived that time. Libby spent every day since, wondering how long it would take before he would get sick again. She tried not to dwell on the idea but found herself wondering about it often, until one day she noticed he was losing weight again. She would later learn that Clovis hadn't told anyone outside his family yet as they wanted privacy. This is the reason she couldn't bring herself to disturb them. His family was there with him now.

"Are you okay?" Libby heard a voice say. She turned to see an older version of a young girl she recalled from middle school, wearing a nurse's uniform. The full-figured familiar woman with her dark hair in a long braid had a look of concern.

Abigail something, recalled Libby. The woman's last name escaping her in the moment.

"Oh dear," Nurse Abigail said. "What happened to you?"

Libby instinctively touched her face, recalling how she

looked. The swelling in her left eye was nearly all gone but not the bruising. Almost half her face was a mixture of yellow, purple and dark red. She looked horrible.

"Rough day at the office," Libby replied.

"I'd say," Nurse Abigail replied. "What kind of office do you work at?"

"I'm a cop," Libby replied seriously.

"Oh! I'm sorry to be so forward. I normally wouldn't be, but I remember you from school. Libby, right? You were a pretty tough kid."

Libby started to smile but was reminded of her facial injuries by a jolt of pain, making her wince.

"Are you related?" Abigail asked, gesturing towards room 305.

"He's my boss," Libby replied. "How is he?"

"He's okay for now," Abigail replied. "He's resting. From what I understand, he'll be released today, maybe tomorrow."

"But for how long?" Libby asked longingly.

"I didn't know if you knew how sick he really is," Abigail replied as she glanced about and lowered her voice so no one could hear her. "He's really very sick."

"Oh, I know. I'll come back to see him tomorrow," Libby stated.

"It was nice seeing you again," Nurse Abigail stated as she pivoted and returned to work.

Just then, the door to room 305 opened and a nurse walked out carrying a covered tray. Through the closing door, Libby made eye contact with Raylene who looked at her with a shocked expression. Raylene burst from room 305 and marched up to Libby.

"Oh my God! Look at you!" Raylene put her hand to her mouth to hide the shock. "Does it hurt?"

Libby smiled slightly, masking the pain as best she could.

"I'd heard you got hurt out there, but oh my God!"

Raylene's expression again reminding Libby how badly bruised she was.

"I'm a little sore but going to be fine," Libby replied. "How's Clovis?"

"Very tired but better now," Raylene's shoulders sagged as she spoke.

"I'm going to need to talk to him about what happened out at Eli's property," Libby stated businesslike, trying not to show emotion.

Raylene took Libby's hands in hers as she pleaded.

"Can this please wait until tomorrow morning? I want him to rest some more so he can get out of the hospital. If all goes well, you can come by the house in the morning. I'm sure he'll love to see you. It will make him feel like he's still working, even if he knows he's no longer allowed," Raylene said with a strained smile.

Libby could see Raylene's smile was forced, trying hard to put on a brave front.

Libby forced her own smile in return, bearing both the physical and emotional pain as best she could.

"Sure. I need to wrap my head around what happened, so I was planning to start with Dwayne anyway," Libby lied.

"Thank you, Libby. I knew you'd understand," Raylene said, hugging Libby hard.

83

"Nurse!" a red-faced Garth barked loudly from his hospital bed. "You need to move me to another room!"

Garth lay in the bed nearest the window showing nothing but a bright blue cloudless sky. His right leg bandaged and elevated in a sling.

"I'm sorry," Nurse Abigail replied as she entered the room. "I can't do that," she said with a warm smile.

"You can't be serious that I have to share a room with this guy?" Garth pointed a thumb at the other bed in the hospital room.

"What's wrong, Garth?" Dwayne asked from his own hospital bed. "You don't want to share a room with a fellow gunshot victim?"

Officer Dwayne Adams lay in the room's second hospital bed, his left shoulder and arm bandaged.

Nurse Abigail smiled at the quip, checked Dwayne's IV and left the room, crossing paths with Libby again.

"Two for one," Libby stated as she entered the hospital room to expressions of shock from the two men.

"Who the hell did that to you?" Garth asked.

"Geez! You look terrible," Dwayne stated.

"You're not exactly looking all that great yourself, sunshine," Libby joked while changing the subject. "And you, Garth. The doc tells me the bullet went through your calf muscle."

"I'm gonna sue," Garth said in a much calmer tone than Libby had anticipated.

"Sue for what?" Libby asked. "The Chief shot you, sure. But he did it to save your life."

"The shotgun was loaded with birdshot," Garth stated with an air of confidence in his voice, as if it wouldn't have been lethal at the range Eli was at the time.

"The Chief saved your life," Dwayne added. "Square on, that could have killed you."

"It doesn't matter," Garth replied bitterly. "He shot me in the leg."

"Will that be your official statement?" Libby asked, looking at Garth.

"Will Eli be pressing charges against Garth?" Dwayne asked Libby.

"Charges against me?" Garth said exuberantly. "That old fucker tried to shoot me."

Libby looked over at Garth as she replied to Dwayne's question.

"I'm not sure yet, considering but I think Ernie will be pursuing something on his own."

"I didn't do anything to Ernie," Garth muttered, sounding defeated. "A little trash in his parking lot isn't exactly a big deal."

"Actually, as it turns out, Eli signed over his property to

Ernie a while ago and so technically you've been littering on Ernie's property and not Eli's."

"Oooh," Dwayne said, his voice filled with delight.

"I'll come back in an hour or two and take official statements from the both of you. I need all the details of what happened. Don't go anywhere," Libby said sarcastically as she left the room to get the things needed to take an official statement.

But first she had one more visit to make.

84

What was left of the front deck on Eli Woodman's home had been cordoned off with caution tape as it was no longer safe. Someone had gone as far as to remove the stairs so old Eli wouldn't stubbornly try and use the front door anyway and hurt himself in the process. For this reason, Officer Libby Terwilliger knocked on Eli Woodman's back door.

While waiting, Libby examined the back stoop she stood on which wasn't in much better shape than the front steps. But since it was just a simple few steps and a small platform, she felt it safe enough for her at this time.

Libby knocked again, this time much louder.

"Ernie? Eli? I know you're in there," Libby remarked as Eli's Fargo and Ernie's car were both in the driveway. "It's Officer Libby Terwilliger and I'm here officially."

A shuffling sound came from inside and then the door opened suddenly. Ernie stood behind the door and had a look of annoyance about him, thought Libby.

"Come in," Ernie said in a bitter tone, his eyes downcast avoiding eye contact.

As Libby entered the dimly lit kitchen, she saw Eli wearing a yellow stained, white t-shirt sitting at the old white marbled Formica table, sipping from an old, battered tin cup. Ernie sat in the chair next to his aging father and placed a hand on the old man's forearm. Libby couldn't help but think this was his way of politely asking his patriarch to let him do the talking.

"Mind if I sit down?" Libby asked.

"The chair's there, ain't it?" Eli mumbled, avoiding eye contact as well.

Libby saw Ernie gently squeeze his father's forearm.

"Before you say anything, I need to record this conversation since I have no witnesses with me," Libby remarked as she set her cellphone down and hit record on a voice recorder app.

Still clutching his father's forearm, Ernie nodded approval.

"I'm Officer Libby Terwilliger at the Woodman residence on Short Fir Road. I'm here with both Eli and Ernie Woodman," Libby said and before she could continue, Eli cut her off.

"I told Clovis to find that som-bitch who was dumpin trash on my property," Eli stated, finally looking her in the eye.

Libby saw Ernie give his father's arm another gentle squeeze.

"Look, Libby," Ernie said sternly, staring at the bruises on her face. "We all know what kind of man Garth is. And we all know, without a doubt that he was the one spreading trash on my father's land."

"Isn't this your land now, Ernie?" Libby asked.

"Yeah-yeah, whatever. It's mine. Yes. Dad signed it over a few years ago when he started forgetting things. We were afraid his siblings might try and lay claim to it, if something happened to him, on account he'd inherited from his father."

Siblings, wondered Libby? How old are they, she wondered? Plus, she didn't think it worked like that but didn't see the point of saying anything.

The father and son exchanged glances before Ernie continued.

"Dad's been getting more and more forgetful. He doesn't always remember giving me the property. But he was just trying to keep trespassers off his... I mean, our land."

"I see," Libby replied while looking at Ernie. "So why didn't you tell us that your father had another shotgun in the house?"

"A few years back, I made sure all he had in the house was weak birdshot that Winston made for me," Ernie said, garnering himself a dirty look from Eli. "Winston made me some shells with less powder in them and I swapped the ammo he had while he wasn't looking. He only used it to shoot at birds, rats or squirrels. Any critters that ate his garden."

"I see," Libby repeated.

"Look, I've been trying to convince my father to go live in a home for the last few years. This house is falling apart, plus his memory is fading slowly and I worry about him living here alone. I can't look after him and he knows it."

"I don't need a babysitter," Eli mumbled before sipping from his tin cup.

"He can fend for himself but he's ninety-three and needs someone around all day long, in case something happens," Ernie added. "I can't do that, and neither can my wife."

Libby watched the father and son exchange a stern glance yet again, as if they wordlessly exchange thoughts or something, thought Libby.

"Whether he admits it or not, he needs help. He's getting forgetful and so can't live here alone anymore. Plus, he's becoming a danger to himself, going off half-cocked," Ernie admitted.

"Does your father have any more guns in the house?" Libby asked.

"No," Ernie answered.

"Are you certain he doesn't have any you're not aware of?" Libby asked while looking at Eli, gauging his reaction.

"I can assure you, he does not," Ernie replied as he straightened in his chair.

Libby could see a look of annoyance on the grocery store manager's face.

"Are we done here? My boy should be home from school at any minute now and I don't want him to see no cops at my house," Eli said glancing back and forth between Libby and Ernie.

"He's getting more and more confused. I'm going to be getting him into Sleepy Meadows as soon as I can," Ernie said, referring to the local nursing home.

Eli set his tin cup down hard, making a dull clunk sound. He glanced bitterly at his son and then back at Libby.

"What was your name again?" a red face Eli asked Libby.

"Are you going to be pressing charges against Garth?" Libby asked while looking at Ernie.

"Yes. I think I will," Ernie replied. "I'm thinking he needs to learn a lesson."

"You'll have to come down to the station for that," Libby stated. "But for now, I'd like to talk about the events from two nights ago. The night I got this," Libby said, pointing to the bruises on her face. "And since I wasn't there to see it myself, I need you to help me get a clearer picture of what happened in the woods. Do you understand me, Eli?"

Eli glanced at Ernie before turning his attention to Libby.

"What do you mean? Two nights ago, I was at the fair with my boy," Eli remarked before sipping the last of the content of his tin cup.

"Two nights ago, you tried to shoot your neighbor Garth Blackett but instead shot Officer Dwayne Adams," Libby stated, leaning forward and glaring at Eli.

"I don't understand," Eli muttered.

"My father's confused," Ernie stated. "His short-term memory isn't what it used to be and he tends to block traumatic events."

"How convenient," Libby mumbled quietly.

"What was that?" Ernie inquired, cocking an ear.

"I need a drink," Eli blurted while looking into his

empty cup. "You. Whatever your name is," Eli said to Ernie. "Pour an old man a drink," Eli said holding out his cup to his son.

"We're out of rum," Ernie replied while reaching for the cup.

"Never mind," Eli said angrily, struggling to get up from his chair. Once on his feet, he staggered over to the sagging kitchen cupboards, opened a creaking door and pulled a half full pint of spiced rum.

Ernie slumped in his chair and sighed.

"You ever find out who threw paint all over the rainbow crosswalk?" Ernie asked, obviously referring to the crosswalk in front of the church.

"Not yet," Libby said, wondering if she should have even said this much.

Eli poured rum in his cup, put the bottle back where he'd gotten it and sat down at the table again.

"Some people think it was the same vandals who burned the town limit sign," Ernie added.

Libby smiled, feeling the pain in her bruised face a little less each time.

"I can't discuss ongoing investigations," Libby replied, thinking of what Clovis would say in this situation.

"So, are you going to charge my father or not?" Ernie asked bluntly as he watched his father sip rum.

"You're telling me he has no memory of trying to shoot Garth Blackett?" Libby asked coldly.

"He's getting more and more confused as time goes on," Ernie stated again as he looked Libby in the eyes. "He's got good days and bad days but he's not always acting rationally. You can't put a ninety-three-year-old in prison. What he needs is a home with full time caregivers."

Eli farted loudly, scratched his shoulder through the t-shirt and sipped rum.

"Can you guarantee there are no more guns in the house?" Libby asked.

"Yes," Ernie replied firmly.

"And do I need to take his keys away? He clearly

shouldn't be driving in this condition," Libby asked.

Eli sank the rest of his rum and set his cup down hard, making a loud clunking noise. He gave Libby a cold hard stare with his one good eye but said nothing.

"I'll take the keys to the truck with me when I leave," Ernie replied meekly.

"To the tractor too?" Libby asked.

"Yes," Ernie answered.

"Som-bitch," Eli muttered.

"Are you going to leave him home alone?" Libby asked, watching their reactions closely, wishing she was videotaping this instead of merely audio recording.

Ernie sighed.

Eli struggled to his feet, staggered slightly as he made his way to the cupboard again and proceeded to pour rum into his tin cup.

"I'm going to make a few calls," Ernie replied. "You know anyone who can pull a few strings?"

Libby knew Ernie was referring to Officer Dwayne Adams whose wife Maureen worked at the nursing home in question. And odds were good, she couldn't help Ernie get his father in any sooner. Although she might have an inside scoop on availabilities and how long the wait list was for starters.

"I'll make a few calls for you," Libby stated as she turned off the recording app on her phone.

"You still have my number?" Ernie inquired, getting up from the table at the same time as Libby.

"I do," Libby replied, thinking back to the last time they threw a birthday bash for Chief Clovis. Recalling how she got contact numbers for a lot of people, including Ernie Woodman. "I'll call you with an update shortly."

Libby pocketed her phone and took another glance at the father and son duo as she took her leave.

Soon she would be on the phone with Maureen Adams asking questions about the Sleepy Meadows nursing home. This would help her decide whether or not to arrest the ninety-three-year-old or not. If he suddenly found himself in a home with full time supervision and no access to a vehicle or guns, then the pressure to lock up the old man would lessen. And she felt it necessary to resist the urge to ask Chief Clovis for help with this. He, if anyone, needed to know the law in this town would be in good hands. He needs to know that she will use her wisdom on how to handle things and not just try and use the law as a hammer.

Sure, the old man tried to shoot someone. Sure, he missed and accidentally shot someone else. But was he of sound mind? Did he really understand what he was doing? This is without a doubt what his lawyer would argue. Libby knew she should arrest the old man. Half the town would argue that she should as he was dangerous. But if he was in Sleepy Meadows, monitored around the clock and didn't have access to guns, this would buy her some time. She needed to pull some strings, she thought as she dialed a number and put the phone on speaker as she drove.

"Maureen?" Libby said when she heard the call get answered. "It's me, Libby. Look, I need some advice."

Part 25

Can't...

85

AS DAYLIGHT WANED, UNDER GREY clouds that threatened rain, Mayor Jack Leger and Bonnie Campbell strolled down the sidewalk, arm in arm.

"Let's go this way," Bonnie stated, tugging Jack so he would turn the corner he would have otherwise walked past.

Jack sighed and gave in to Bonnie's wishes, walking along the street where the houses were still covered in Christmas decorations.

"Thank you for dinner," Bonnie said, kissing Jack on the cheek.

"It *was* nice to go out," Jack replied.

"And be seen?"

Jack smiled and patted Bonnie's arm with his free hand.

"I told you nobody would make a fuss about us," Bonnie commented.

"I just assume some will."

"Why? You've been a widower for a long time now. It's okay for you to live, even if you lost your wife, Jack."

"I know, but you know how judgmental some are."

"Your happiness is none of their business."

"Ah but some will have something to say about it," Jack stated as he paused in his tracks and admired the unlit Christmas decorations of the first home from the row.

"So?" Bonnie asked.

"So, I'm the mayor," Jack replied.

"You worry too much about what people will say about your personal life," Bonnie said with an air of annoyance. "Besides, it's my life too. My friends will tease me about my getting involved with a younger man," Bonnie said with a smile.

The couple walked quietly for a moment, still arm in arm until they were passing the Musgrave house.

"That's odd," Jack stated. "Ms. Musgrave should have turned on her lights by now."

"Seriously, Jack?" Bonnie asked, not at all hiding her look of disbelief.

"What?"

"Nobody's turned their lights on for the last two nights. Not since Clovis went in the hospital again."

Jack shrugged, trying to give Bonnie his best, I didn't know look.

"I can't help but wonder about you, Mr. Mayor, who seems to be up on all the town gossip and yet you can be so damned clueless sometimes. Ms. Musgrave's lights have always been for Clovis and Raylene. They met at Christmas, a long time ago and so it's always been very special to them."

"I always wonder how you know all these things?" Jack asked.

"I pay attention," Bonnie replied with smugness in her voice. "Plus, Raylene and I are friends."

"I heard Cotton is home," Jack replied proudly, hoping he had gossip that Bonnie didn't yet know.

"I know," Bonnie replied. "Raylene told me he wasn't supposed to be home for a few more months, but he was sent home early since his father was ill."

Strolling slowly again, admiring the unlit Christmas decorations, the couple walked on.

"Have you seen Libby?" Bonnie asked.

"Yes. It's been a week and a half since she took a brick to the face and the bruising is only starting to fade now."

"I saw her with Reggie earlier today. He's looking better too," Bonnie stated.

"He was banged up but is doing better. Dwayne though, is still out for a bit."

"I would hope so, after being shot," Bonnie grimaced.

"Eli only grazed him and with birdshot too," Jack stated as if that should make it less important.

"You can't graze someone with a shotgun," Bonnie said. "Sure, only some of the scatter hit him but still. He got shot."

Jack shrugged, not wanting to argue over semantics that wouldn't change the facts anyway.

At the end of the string of decorated houses, Bonnie stopped and helped Jack turn around so they could walk past the row of festive homes once more.

"You think Clovis will be released from the hospital again?" Jack inquired.

"I can't see it happening this time," Bonnie said, her voice breaking with emotion. "Clovis isn't recovering this time."

Jack patted Bonnie's hand, showing the only kind of emotional support he knew. Jack cleared his throat and tried to divert the subject away from the topic of the beloved chief of police dying of cancer.

"Eli Woodman's finally starting to get used to living in Sleepy Meadows," Jack stated.

"I heard he snuck outside on the first day, tried to steal a truck," Bonnie said, clearly suppressing a giggle.

"It's not funny," Jack said, struggling to keep a straight face. "He's ninety-three and still quite feisty. They say he's confused but Maureen told me he's still pretty darned sharp for his age."

"Well, he can't go home anymore," Bonnie stated. "Not since Ernie got Garth to bulldoze his father's old house."

"I know," Jack said with renewed excitement in his voice. "Word is Ernie made a deal with Garth. If Garth cleaned the trash he's dumped on his property and bulldozed the old house for free, he'd not press charges."

"Lucky for Garth," Bonnie said with smile. "And that house really was falling apart anyway."

"Ernie said he was afraid of something bad happening as it was in such a bad state."

"Something did happen. The deck collapsed on Reggie plus the chimney fell over and almost killed Libby," Bonnie said.

"Speaking of Libby, she's going to take over as interim chief."

"She'd make a great chief," Bonnie replied. "Although she's got really big shoes to fill."

"I think she's too young," Jack stated. "I think she needs more experience to be Chief."

"I know she's young in your eyes, but Clovis taught her well. And she is the best candidate for the job."

"I know that. I just think she's too young to take over for good, although she agreed to take over for now."

"You're being an ass. You only say that because she's a woman," Bonnie said firmly.

"Heck no!" Jack barked. He stopped walking and glared at Bonnie. "She's a great cop but I'm not sure she's cut out to be chief is what I'm saying." Jack started walking at a brisker pace this time, making Bonnie pick up the pace to keep up.

"I can't believe you, sometimes," Jack muttered bitterly.

They turned a street corner and started heading back the way they'd come.

"She should have charged Eli, no matter if he's losing his mind or not," Jack insisted.

"Slow down," Bonnie said tugging Jack's arm.

Jack stopped and looked at Bonnie.

"Hit a nerve, did I?" Bonnie asked.

"He tried to shoot a man," Jack said with an angry tone.

"She may still pursue charges," Bonnie replied. "Who knows? But he's no longer a danger to anyone now."

Jack and Bonnie began a slow stroll again.

"Ernie said since the house was torn down, his father's

taken a liking to his new home," Bonnie added.

"He should." Jack smiled. "Old Eli's getting treated like a king now."

Bonnie smiled.

"Although he keeps asking the staff to get him rum," Jack added.

"Maureen told me Eli's flirting with all the ladies," Bonnie replied. "He's like a kid again. She also said that Eli's not as confused as they first let on."

"It's probably just the fact that he's sober now."

Bonnie huffed before she spoke.

"Eli wasn't a real alcoholic. Trust me. He drank, sure. But not as much as people say."

"And how would you know that?" Jack inquired.

"I've got friends in the liquor dispensing business," Bonnie stated.

Jack gently tugged Bonnie's arm as they reached the corner, indicating his desire to head back the way they'd come. The couple turned and continued their stroll in what was quickly becoming late evening. Nearby, in the now somber night, a streetlight flickered and then came on.

"Have you heard anything about who threw paint on the rainbow crosswalk?" Bonnie asked.

Jack huffed. "Never mind that. What I want to know is who burned down the town limit sign?"

"Some people say it's the same person who did both," Bonnie stated confidently.

"It's not," Jack replied.

"What about those kids who you saw vandalizing the Christmas decorations?"

"What about them?"

"It could be them; wouldn't you think?"

"Don't be writing articles based on guesses again," Jack said angrily.

"I'll write whatever I darned well please," Bonnie stated indignantly. "It's my newspaper."

"Yes, but you can't do opinion pieces on who may have

committed a crime. You've no proof of any of it. Rumors are not proof."

Bonnie smiled as they turned off the sidewalk and walked up the cobblestone path that led to the front door of her home.

"Coffee, tea… or me?" Bonnie said with a smile and a wink.

Part 26

Lord, Give Us Strength.

86

WEARING JEANS AND A CHECKERED flannel shirt, Libby sat in a firm chair of a small dimly lit family room near the palliative care facility of Stonevalley Hospital. Clutched in her hands were wads of damp tissues which she used to dab at the steady stream of tears.

"Are you okay?" she heard a familiar voice ask.

Through blurry teary eyes, she saw Father Finnigan in full black priest garb, standing in the doorway. For the briefest of moments, Libby wondered if she had ever seen Father Finnigan wearing anything other than his black clothes with his clerical collar. Perhaps he wore priest's robes in church, but Libby never attended mass. Of course, with the upcoming funeral, that would change soon she thought, bringing on fresh tears.

"My-my," Father Finnigan said as he sat in the chair next to Libby. "You love him very much. That's clear to see."

"I hate seeing him like that," Libby replied, her voice cracking with emotion.

"I know it can be hard watching someone we love fade away like that," Father Finnigan said as he pulled a rosary from his pocket and slipped the blessed beads through his fingers.

"I can't do it anymore. I'm not strong enough," Libby said dabbing away fresh tears.

Father Finnigan rested a hand on Libby knee as he spoke.

"We have to be strong, for Raylene and the children."

"That woman is incredible," Libby stated while trying to compose herself.

"This is the second time for her. She was convinced Clovis wouldn't survive the first time he had cancer." Father Finnigan returned to a rhythmic handling of the rosary, running it through his fingers a few beads at a time. "They made the best of the time they had after that."

"He was a changed man," Libby replied. "It was as if he didn't care about a lot of things anymore."

"I wouldn't say he didn't care," Father Finnigan replied. "I'd say he stopped spending time on things he felt were frivolous. Things that didn't merit a lot of attention, in his opinion."

"We don't all agree on what's frivolous," Libby replied in a serious tone. "He should have taken the situation between Garth and Eli a lot more seriously, in *my* opinion."

"I'm sure Clovis had his reasons," Father Finnigan replied.

"Mind if I come in?" Libby heard a meek voice inquire.

Ms. Musgrave stood at the door, leaning on a cane while clutching a small pink purse that matched her dress.

"Please, sit with us," Father Finnigan replied with a forced smile.

"My hip pains me when I stand too long now," Ms. Musgrave stated. Staggering slightly, she shuffled to the closest chair and plopped in it with a sigh. "Getting old is horrible," she added.

"Getting old is a privilege," Libby stated, trying to keep herself from getting emotional again.

"It's God's plan," Father Finnigan interjected.

Libby glared at him for a moment, wondering what about someone being made to suffer so much at the end of his life would do for God. But she decided that she would resist saying anything about this. Whenever she talked about such things, it only brought back memories of

Thinking-Lincoln and the incident at Burnett's Place. Thinking about that still gave Libby a queasy feeling in the pit of her stomach.

"I just had to come see him," Ms. Musgrave said softly. "I've been wanting to but since I fell, I've not been able to get around as much as I used to."

"Would you have room for two more?" Libby heard someone ask.

At the door of the small family room, stood Bonnie Campbell and Mayor Jack Ledger. The little room had ten chairs in total.

"I don't think he's got much longer," Bonnie said in a soft tone that wasn't her usual self.

Jack took her arm and led her to chairs where they sat together.

"It feels like much of Carlton is already in mourning," Father Finnigan stated while glancing about the room.

"He was loved by many," Bonnie added.

"His mother was a dear friend of mine," Ms. Musgrave commented.

"I was afraid once he retired from the force, he'd run against me as mayor," Jack said, grimacing as he said it.

Libby figured he'd realized what he said when it came out of his mouth. Sounding as if he was glad the beloved Carlton native who ran the police force for all these years wouldn't run against him in an election. But Libby knew that in Jack's mind, this was supposed to be a compliment for him to see Clovis as a worthy adversary in local politics.

"Ahem!"

Libby heard someone clearing their throat. With a glance at the door, she saw Winston who owned the Pinewood Lodge. He was a good friend of Chief Clovis's, she thought. From behind Winston, Officer Dwayne Adams peeked into the room.

"Hey," Dwayne said as he took off his cap and entered the now crowded room.

In a moment of quiet, they heard a voice at the door.

"From the looks of things, I'd say there's nobody left in Carlton right now."

At the door stood Raylene McPhee, tears in her eyes and a small smile on her lips.

Bonnie was the first to get to her for a hug, towering over the short wife of the beloved chief of police. She was quickly followed by Libby.

"Thank you all for coming," Raylene spoke, her voice filled with sadness.

"Dear, how is he?" Ms. Musgrave inquired as she struggled to her feet.

Raylene hugged the old caring woman hard.

"Thank you for everything you did for us," Raylene said to Ms. Musgrave. "You brought us a lot of joy in a time when we needed it most." Raylene held Ms. Musgrave to her as she continued. "Clovis passed away about an hour ago."

Libby struggled to contain a sob of emotion as she heard the news.

"I'm so sorry," Winston said.

"Let's say a prayer," Officer Dwayne Adams said. "Father? Would you, please?"

Some held hands, others held each other as Father Finnigan began a prayer.

Part 27

The Carlton Gazette Memoriam

87

Police Chief Clovis McPhee Remembered

At the age of fifty-seven, with his family at his side, Police Chief Clovis McPhee lost his battle with cancer on August 23rd. He will be sadly missed by his wife, Raylene (Allison) McPhee, son Cotton McPhee and daughter Anna McPhee. Born and raised in Carlton, he was the youngest son of the late Patrick McPhee and Margret (Driscoll) McPhee, he had one brother, George McPhee who died tragically in a traffic accident at the age of thirty-two.

At the age of twenty, Clovis had left Carlton to fulfill a childhood dream of becoming a police officer. He spent his early years on the force as a patrolman in Poplar Falls followed by a short stint in Maple Springs, where he would meet his future wife, Raylene. From there he transferred to the police force in Stonevalley, where he rose in the ranks and at the age of forty, he moved back to his hometown of Carlton to become police chief in what he lovingly referred to as a sleepy little town. And as one of Carlton's own, Chief

Clovis McPhee found himself in a position of authority in the very town he had grown up in. Soon people learned that he wouldn't be one to lord over the townsfolk. He was one of them, always standing with the citizens during trying times. He showed compassion and understanding as often as he could. A kind man who on many occasions, if the situation allowed, lent a helping hand instead of dolling out punishment. Clovis always looked for solutions instead of pointing fingers or laying blame. As a leader in the community, he enforced the law when it was called for with a just and fair hand. And even though he was considered a lawman who could have easily put himself ahead of everyone, often he acted in a selfless manor. He was involved in the community and people loved him for it.

Clovis, along with town council, helped start a local youth's baseball team with the goal of helping local kids focus on character building activities. He helped teach kids comradery and helped them feel like they belonged in the community.

Clovis McPhee wasn't just Carlton's Chief of Police; he was a beloved son, husband, father and a dear friend to many. He will be missed.

Father Finnigan has asked us to mention that a special mass will be held next Saturday in honor of the late Clovis McPhee and his family. All will be welcome.

88

JACK LEDGER FOLDED HIS copy of the Carlton Gazette and set it down on the kitchen table. He cleared his throat, sipped tea from his almost empty mug and wiped away a tear as he spoke.

"That's the first time I see an obituary on the front page of a newspaper."

Bonnie, who sat across the table, set down her multigrain toast and pushed the plate forward a little as she replied.

"I couldn't very well not put the death of the Chief of Police on the front page. And it would have felt weird to write an article and then have a separate obituary in the back pages too. So, I combined the two."

"I suppose," Jack stated. "You have a point."

"I wanted to write a much longer article about his life, but Raylene asked me not to." Her empty teacup in hand, Bonnie got up, took Jack's cup and headed into the kitchen.

"It's your paper," Jack replied. "You could have written something longer if you wanted to."

"Of course. But Raylene is my friend, and she lost her husband. I wasn't going to do something to upset her more than I had to. I mean I couldn't not do a feature on Clovis. Everyone in town expected it."

Bonnie made more tea as she continued.

"Besides. I did a pictorial tribute in the middle of the paper. A double page pictorial in honor of the late chief of police."

Jack unfolded the paper and flipped to the middle page. There were seven pictures of Chief Clovis in uniform at various joyous events as well as past tragedies. Jack quietly marveled at the pictures as Bonnie returned with more tea. She set a cup down in front of Jack as she spoke.

"That's the last one, by the way."

"The last what?" Jack asked as he refolded the paper and sipped hot tea.

"That's the last printed edition of the Carlton Gazette."

"Really?"

"I should have stopped printing months ago but when I came to realize this day was coming, I kept going. I wanted *this* edition to be the last printed one."

"This one?" Jack asked, gesturing at the copy on the table.

"The one with Clovis' obituary."

"Ah. Okay. But are you sure you want to stop printing?"

"I'm losing money already, and it will only get worse if I keep on printing," Bonnie replied. "The paper isn't making enough money. Besides, people don't read the paper anymore. They get all their news on Facebook."

Jack frowned, shook his head, sipped tea and fiddled with the paper.

"If I publish online only, it will allow me to keep it running for a while longer," Bonnie stated. "I'm hoping I can keep it profitable long enough for me to make it to retirement."

"Then what?" Jack inquired. "What happens to the paper then?"

"I don't know," Bonnie replied. "If it's making a little money, maybe I sell it. If not, maybe I shut it down."

Jack grunted and sipped tea.

"Newspapers aren't as profitable as they used to be," Bonnie stated as she sipped tea. "Especially not small ones like The Carlton Gazette."

Part 28

Interim Chief and Sleepless Nights

89

ON A COOL, QUIET FALL evening, as the sun disappeared behind the colorful autumn trees, Interim Chief Libby Terwilliger stopped her cruiser on the roadside in Pleasant Ridge. In the glow of her headlights was the new town limit sign. The city council had had it replaced two weeks after Chief Clovis McPhee had passed away. Angered by this, Libby's first instinct was to burn the damned thing, same as the previous one which had been burnt. But having publicly vocalized her displeasure about it being replaced after Clovis' passing, she wasn't convinced she would be able to get away with it. Besides, she felt it was a wiser decision to resist the urge to burn this one. Although she couldn't leave it untouched. She pulled a small black duffel bag from the floor on the passenger side. From the bag, Libby pulled out a can of black spray-paint and got out of the cruiser.

On the new decorative wood town limit sign, Libby spray painted *Population 1219* (based on the most recent census), then painted a line across the number and replaced it with *1218*, written in the same black paint.

Libby stood back with her balled up fists on her hips and admired her work.

In that moment, Libby saw headlights heading her way. She stood fast and waited for the approaching car to pass, only it slowed as it got to her.

The truck now at a crawl, came to a stop in the road. The driver was Winston.

"Evening," Winston said to Libby as he nodded, adjusted his baseball cap and leaned against the open driver side window of his truck.

"Evening," Libby replied, suddenly realizing that she still held the spray paint in her hand.

"What's the trouble?" Winston asked.

"Someone painted the new sign," Libby replied, gesturing towards it with the hand still holding the spray paint. She followed Winston's eye to the can in her hand.

"I see that," Winston stated.

"Found this over by the bushes over there," Libby lied, gesturing towards a nearby wild bush.

"Looks pretty fresh," Winston stated.

"That it does. You meet any oncoming traffic on your way down the ridge?" Libby asked.

"Nope. Ain't seen nobody but you."

Libby could see Winston was still eyeballing the spray paint in her hand.

"I probably shouldn't have touched it with my bare hands," Libby said while looking at the spray paint. "It being evidence and all."

"Probably not," Winston replied.

"I guess I got a little excited," Libby added. "They probably wore gloves anyway."

"Probably so," Winston replied.

"I doubt I ever find who painted this," Libby lied again.

"Probably not," Winston agreed. "Well, good luck anyway."

Libby watched as Winston drove off, leaving her standing in the headlights of her cruiser, before the vandalized town limit sign. And she couldn't help but wonder what people would say when Winston told them the story of what he had seen.

Most would talk about how Libby was inexperienced enough to pick up the paint can with her bare hands. Surely, she should know better, they'd say. And some would say that she wasn't cut out to be chief, even if it was just in interim. She lacked the intuition. She lacked the gut instincts that usually comes with grey hair and years of paying attention. But strangely, she felt herself at ease with the idea that people would think her not capable of being chief. It would allow her a certain amount of leeway, she thought. Like just now, with Winston. She doubted that he would even think she could have been lying.

Or could he?

Winston was one of the people who told her she would make a great chief. Now she had made him believe she was incompetent. Well maybe not incompetent. Brash, thought Libby. He'd think me brash. Acting without thinking. Inexperienced, maybe.

"Ah the hell with it," Libby said as she got in her cruiser. She plopped the paint can on top of the duffel bag and sat staring at the defaced signed.

I got away with painting the sign the first time, she pondered. So why couldn't I get away with it again? My therapist said I needed to let my feelings out. So, the first time was to commemorate the ones who died in the Burnett incident, all those years ago. This time it was to commemorate her mentor, Chief Clovis McPhee. A man who had showed her what it was to be a good person while still being a flawed human. He never tried to be perfect. Just good and she loved him for that. As she drove off, leaving the sign in her rearview mirror, her thoughts wandered to her appointment in the morning. It was long overdue, she thought. Plus, it would have made Clovis happy.

90

"IT'S BEEN A WHILE since you've been in to see me," Doctor Evee Melanson said to Libby.

Libby sat in the middle of the couch across from Doctor Melanson's chair in the bright office. The curtains on the large windows were fully opened for a change, letting in the vibrant uplifting energy of the morning sun.

Officer Libby Terwilliger wore jeans and a pink V neck top which gave her a casual appearance, a sharp contrast to the doctor's dark grey blazer and matching pants. The office was neat as usual, noticed Libby. Just like before.

"It's been almost three months since I last saw you. How have you been?" Doctor Melanson inquired.

"Good," Libby replied. "Busy," she added.

"I have to admit, I didn't think I'd ever see you in my office again."

"Why's that?" Libby asked, puzzled.

"I hope you don't mind my saying, but you only came to see me because Chief McPhee made you."

Libby smiled.

"Well turns out he was right about that. I needed to talk to someone about what had happened."

"You still can't say it?"

"What happened at Burnett's Place," Libby muttered halfheartedly.

"Progress," Doctor Melanson replied. "You've never said the name of the place where it happened out loud in my office before."

"I'm getting better," Libby said, her expression now serious. She shifted in her seat to get rid of some of the nervous energy she suddenly felt. "He was right. I needed to talk to someone who would have an open mind. Not judge me. Someone I could trust. Someone who would keep my secrets."

"Well, I'm glad you came back," Doctor Melanson said, crossing her legs and intertwining her fingers.

"Too many sleepless nights. I needed to talk to someone before I exploded."

"What's on your mind?"

"Where do I start?"

"Wherever you'd like. You're my only appointment today so it's okay if we take longer."

"So much has happened since the last time I came to see you," Libby sank in the couch a little as she continued.

"I'm interim Chief now, did you know that?"

"I'd heard."

"Some people want me to take over for good," Libby said, watching Doctor Melanson's body language out of habit.

"How do you feel about that?"

"I've mixed feelings about it," Libby said, turning to look outside at the colorful fall leaves on the trees.

"How so?"

"Well, I don't want the pressure that comes with the responsibilities," Libby said turning her attention back to the doctor. "I don't know if I can handle it, for one thing."

"You're more capable than you give yourself credit for. Clovis knew that," Doctor Melanson stated.

"How would you know that?"

"He told me. Long ago. When he first called me about you."

"Are you supposed to tell me that?" Libby asked.

"Clovis is passed away now. And it's okay for me to tell you that he thought highly of you."

"Sometimes I feel like I'll never be good enough."

"You are."

"Sure. But I will never be as good a chief as Clovis was."

"Perhaps. Perhaps not. Only one way to find out, isn't there?"

"I don't know if I want the job, but I also know I don't want an outsider to come and take over either." Libby sighed before continuing. "Reggie or Dwayne won't be applying for the job. And a lot of people are looking at me for it. As if I'm supposed to want it."

"Do you?"

"The mayor, Jack Ledger doesn't want me to apply."

"Does that bother you?" Doctor Melanson asked.

"A little. Maybe. I don't know. He hasn't come out and said it to my face, but I know."

"Perhaps you're just being paranoid."

"I'm not."

"I'm not so sure," Doctor Melanson said with a tilt of

her head that spoke volumes.

Libby could see the doctor did believe her paranoid and so she stated confidently, "I have something on him."

"Oh?"

"He's the one who threw black paint on the rainbow crosswalk in front of the church!" Libby blurted.

"Can you prove it?" Doctor Melanson asked, her voice raising a notch in what Libby read as disbelief.

"I have the lid of the paint can he used. Clovis had it hidden in his office, so I have it now."

"A lid? Does it have fingerprints or something? I mean how would you know it was his?"

"It has tool marks. When it was repeatedly pried open, he left tool marks on the edge of the lid."

"And this is proof that the mayor did it?"

"Yes."

"I don't follow," Doctor Melanson confessed.

"The night Garth Blackett rear-ended Jack Ledger's sedan, the mayor was admiring his handwork. He had slowed to look at the crosswalk and Garth plowed into his sedan with his truck. So Clovis took a bunch of pictures of the accident that night."

Doctor Melanson furrowed her brow as she spoke. "I feel like you're not telling me something."

"I'm not convinced Clovis realized it at the time, but the mayor's trunk was full of stuff for his apartments, including a can of black paint that was missing a lid. And if you zoom into the pictures closely, you can see the matching tool marks from the lid Clovis had previously found at the scene."

"Does anyone else know this?"

"Jack does."

"You told the mayor you knew he committed a crime?"

"I used it as leverage once, when I need something from him."

"Seriously?"

"It wasn't my finest moment," Libby said with a smirk.

"Interesting dilemma you've created for yourself."

"I'm good at self-sabotaging myself."

"I see that."

"Anyway, this is why I know he doesn't want me to become chief permanently. I have something on him and so he couldn't try and manipulate me."

"Does the mayor have a say in who gets the job?"

"He has influence on the decision but it's not up to him."

"So do you want the job?" Doctor Melanson asked again.

"I don't want anyone to replace Clovis," Libby said, pausing to wipe away a tear. "The only way to keep that from happening is if I get the job."

"Sounds like you've already made up your mind."

"Maybe. Oh, and Eli Woodman's faking," Libby replied, suddenly wanting to change the subject before she became emotional.

"You mean Ernie Woodman?"

"Eli. Ernie Woodman's father. He's the old man who shot Dwayne."

"I'm sorry, what?" Doctor Melanson asked.

Libby knew the doctor was confused as she had mentioned a lot of people in her sessions, but Eli was new to her.

"Garth Blackett was dumping trash on his neighbor Eli Woodman's property. Only it turned out that his son Ernie Woodman actually owns the property now. And to get out of going to jail, ninety-three-year-old Eli faked having Alzheimer's."

"And you think this why?" Doctor Melanson asked, shifting in her chair.

"Dwayne's wife works at Sleepy Meadows, the nursing home where Eli is now."

"Dwayne, the officer you work with? The one who got shot?"

"Officer Dwayne Adams, yes. His wife Maureen works at the home."

"Is she a doctor, this Maureen?"

"She's a caregiver," Libby replied.

"I'm not sure that makes her qualified to make such judgments about her wards."

"She didn't actually say she thought he was faking. She just talked about how vibrant he was for his age. Also, how he was flirting with all the women. Although she did mention that he was pretty sharp for a man who's supposed to be getting senile."

"That's not exactly a medical diagnosis," Doctor Melanson said.

"When I interviewed Eli at his house, I could tell something was off," Libby stated. "It was like Eli had been coached by his son, Ernie."

"Cop's intuition?"

"That and I saw Eli wink at Ernie."

"He could have had something in his eye," Doctor Melanson commented.

"Twice."

"Ah."

"I should have arrested him."

"How's Dwayne?" Doctor Melanson inquired.

"Good. He's back to work."

"And Eli? How's he doing?"

"He wasn't too happy about being there but he's better now, ever since they tore down his old house."

"And why'd they tear down his house?"

"It was falling apart. The deck collapsed and the chimney fell on me; knocked me unconscious."

"What?"

"Word is, Ernie is thinking about selling the property. Since his father doesn't live there anymore. I think I might make him an offer."

"Are you sure about that? Doesn't he live next door to Bart who dumped trash on his property?"

"Garth," Libby corrected. "Garth Blackett. He's got his place for sale too. He got fired from the cranberry site and now everyone in town nicknamed him The Trash Man."

"Fitting," Doctor Melanson quipped. Something Libby

thought was a bit out of character for the doctor.

"He put his place up for sale. Word is he's leaving town."

"He's one that could use my counselling," Doctor Melanson stated. "If ever he ends up getting in trouble with the new Chief."

Libby briefly laughed at the idea.

"Now let's back up a little so you can tell me about that chimney knocking you out?" Doctor Melanson asked.

Libby guffawed.

"Yeah. You should've seen my face. I looked horrible," Libby says as she reached for her small purse and took out her phone. She activated it and after a quick search, showed the doctor a selfie of her brick-battered face at its worst.

"Oh my God!" Doctor Melanson exclaimed in shock.

"I know, huh," Libby said. She swiped to the next picture that showed the swelling down but the colorful bruising at its worst.

"That must have hurt," Doctor Melanson said as she moved from her chair to the couch and sat next to Libby to better see the pictures.

Libby swiped twice more, showing more pictures of the healing process and the incredibly colorful bruising of her face. One swipe too far got her to a selfie she took of a gaunt looking Clovis and herself on the first few days of his last hospital stay.

Libby burst into sobs as Doctor Evee Melanson scooped up a box of tissues, holding it at the ready, as if waiting for the sudden bout of emotion to subside.

The End

Author's Note

If you've read my other works, you know that I have written in multiples genres and tend to venture into the darker side of fiction, leaning heavily into the horror genre. On most days, that feels normal to me. However, if you've read a lot of my fiction, you'll see that I have dabbled in many other genres including this one which is drama.

So, why make this novel, which is a sequel to a gory crime thriller novella, a drama?

Why not, I say.

But seriously, I don't always set out with a genre in mind when I begin developing my stories. Although quite often the initial idea may already fit into a category and can already wear a specific label. In this case, I knew the goal of this novel when I sat down to write it. Like I said in the introduction, I simply wanted to go back to Carlton, a place loosely inspired by my hometown, and spend time there. Bask in the company of the residents of this little community.

And just like my last novel, *Maple Springs*, the very first scene I wrote isn't the first scene in the book. Partway into writing it, I realized I needed to write a prologue and foreshadow things to come. And a third of the way into writing this novel, I knew it would be my first full dramatic novel. Mind you, you will find a bit of humor in this book as well. It's quite difficult for me to completely stifle my sense of humor in anything I do. The quarrel between Ms. Musgrave and Mayor Jack Ledger began as what it turns out to be. Quirky. And unbeknownst to the mayor, she is doing this for someone special. The mayor, for his own selfish reasons, has a problem with her recent obsession. But I couldn't not inject humor into this part as the idea alone was funny to me. And while I had decided to write a drama, I also wanted to have parts that would warm your heart and make you smile as well. Most great dramatic stories tend to be a roller coaster of emotions and so I wanted to do just that. But don't read too much into the idea of why this was done. Some spend too much time analyzing the deeper meaning of stories while the author simply loved the characters and wanted to expand on their story arcs.

Also, I feel that I need to mention that not all authors get to write a book in a three-month span and have it published in less than a year. Some might have that ability and tools to do it but most of us don't. I mention this because of the dedication at the beginning of the book. I dedicate this book to my late sister, Diane Comeau who succumbed to cancer in 2024. This wasn't originally intended as I started writing this book just after I finished writing my supernatural horror novel *Maple Springs*. I started this Carlton novel in late 2018 and only submitted it to the publisher in 2022. Books take time for those of us who are still not earning a living off the craft of storytelling. My previously mentioned novel *Maple Springs* was submitted to my publisher in 2019 but was sidelined due to *Oakwood Island: The Awakening* taking precedence. Anyway, I mention this because when I wrote this dramatic novel about loss, I was unaware that before it would see publication, I would lose my sister Diane to cancer. She read all my fiction and would often tell me what she thought of them. I loved hearing her comments and feedback. She may be gone but is not forgotten, hence the dedication.

And one other thing I always mention in my author's notes is the cover of the book. I struggled with this one as most of my ideas were rehashing of previous covers making this one too similar to what I had done before. And while I do have an artistic side and can draw, I don't find my art is good enough for me to illustrate my own book covers. I'm a better cartoonist than an artist and so I know my limits. My photoshop and photography skills can get me covers such as the previously mentioned short story collection *Sleepless Nights*. But I felt I had nothing that I could use that would represent the entire story. I thought about using an old tractor but that would only encompass a small part of the book. Also, the idea of stringing Christmas lights on the tractor was intriguing as well as that would represent other aspects of the tale.

With that said, in comes a real artist, Ian Bristow, recommended by my publisher Geoff Habiger. The cover you see is the results of conversations about the book having a larger cast of characters. And this cover does something I normally don't do, which is put faces on the cover. But it's so different than my usual book covers that it has a sharp contrast to my other works, and I hope you like it.

With all that said, if you're like me and read the book and are now getting to its end, I have to say thank you for letting me entertain you with my stories. It is always a great pleasure and is my goal as a writer. So, until next time.

Best wishes.
Pierre C. Arseneault

About the Author

The youngest of eleven children, Pierre C. Arseneault grew up in the small town of Rogersville, New Brunswick, Canada. As a cartoonist, Pierre was published in over a dozen newspapers. As an author, he has written novels and short stories, both solo and in collaboration. Pierre currently lives in the outskirts of his hometown again, near Rogersville in New Brunswick, Canada.